Frida & Diego

Frida & Diego

ART, LOVE, LIFE

Catherine Reef

CLARION BOOKS

Houghton Mifflin Harcourt

Boston ● New York

Clarion Books is an imprint of Houghton Mifflin Harcourt Publishing Company.

www.hmhco.com

The text was set in Neutraface.

Library of Congress Cataloging-in-Publication Data
Reef, Catherine, author.
Frida & Diego : art, love, life / Catherine Reef.
p. cm.
Includes bibliographical references.
ISBN 978-0-547-82184-9 (hardcover)
1. Kahlo, Frida — Juvenile literature. 2. Rivera, Diego, 1886–1957 — Juvenile literature. 3. Painters — Mexico —
Biography — Juvenile literature. 4. Artist couples — Mexico — Biography — Juvenile literature. I. Title.
ND259.K33R44 2014
759.972 — dc23
[B]
2013021340

Manufactured in China
SCP 10 9 8 7 6 5 4
4500632640

Photograph page ii: Diego Rivera and Frida Kahlo, 1941.

For Francis M. Preziosi,
who loved to paint and loved Mexico

Contents

1

The Artists Wed

················· ❀ ·················

*¡E*SOS CHICOS! Those kids! How dare they play tricks on him and interrupt his work! Diego Rivera was a busy man, and an important one. He was the famous artist who had been hired in 1922 to paint a mural in the auditorium of the National Preparatory School. Black-suited teachers and city officials came often to admire his yellow-clad angels and his haloed saints looking toward the stars. Like the great muralists of the Italian Renaissance, Rivera was painting a religious subject, the Creation, although he claimed not to believe in God.

So why must he put up with these teenagers—these troublemakers—stealing his lunch and rubbing soap on the stairs? How they would giggle to see his great globe of a belly bouncing down the steps. Well, he would tread carefully.

These young people studied at Mexico City's finest high school, but they knew nothing about respect. The worst one was that girl Frida Kahlo, the one whose face shone with mischief. She liked to spy on him while he romanced his pretty models. She would wait until he leaned in for a kiss to shout from her hiding place, "On guard, Diego! Here comes Lupe!" Rivera was soon to marry the striking Lupe Marín, who often kept him company while he painted.

Frida and Diego were photographed on August 21, 1929, their wedding day.

Rivera and Kahlo march in a communist rally prior to their wedding.

This girl even had the nerve to call him by his first name. But she admired his painting; he could tell. Once, when he was working late, she pushed too hard against the auditorium door and almost fell into the room. Straightening up and smoothing her schoolgirl's dress, she asked, "Would it cause you any annoyance if I watched you at work?"

Intrigued, Rivera replied that to the contrary, he would be charmed. So Frida sat for three hours, following every stroke of the artist's brush. Then she said good night and left. Recalling that evening much later, Rivera remarked, "I had no idea that she would one day be my wife."

They met again several years later. No one knows exactly how. One friend remembered them meeting at a party; another friend insisted things happened differently. Frida and Diego both liked to tell the same story, though. It was 1928, and Rivera was finishing an immense project, 124 murals in Mexico's Ministry of Education. Scenes of people at play and at work lined the open corridors around the building's courtyards. He had painted *los tejedores*, weavers at their looms, and *los alfareros*, potters molding jugs. Villages and landscapes spanned doorways. Peasants' portraits and images drawn from myth adorned stairways and elevators.

Rivera was balanced high on a wooden scaffold, applying pigment to wet plaster on a third-floor balcony wall, when a voice broke his concentration. *"¡Diego, baje!"* ("Come down!")

He peered at the speaker standing below. Who was this bold young woman? Rivera had an eye for female beauty. He quickly took in a "fine nervous body, topped by a delicate face." The speaker wore her dark hair long, and her eyes flashed with uncommon fire.

She was twenty-one and spoke and stood with confidence, but it took great energy for her to hold herself together. Three years before, her body had been pierced and shattered in a horrific accident. Her doctors had expected her to die, but she lived. She had only recently left her bed and started venturing into Mexico City again.

FRIDA KAHLO, *SELF-PORTRAIT AS A TEHUANA*, 1943.

Kahlo painted herself wearing a traditional headdress of the Tehuantepec region of Mexico and looking like a somber bride. Rivera's face appears on her forehead; could he have caused her sadness?

Rivera climbed down. More than six feet tall, he loomed over the girl when standing beside her. But she, undaunted, got right to the point. "Look, I have not come to flirt with you or anything," she said, aware of his reputation. She had been painting, she explained, and she wanted him to see what she had done. "If it interests you, tell me so; if it doesn't interest you, likewise, so that I can work at something else."

She showed him three or four canvases, all portraits of women. They were a beginner's work, but Rivera saw in them "a vital sensuality, complemented by a merciless yet sensitive power of observation." He concluded, "It was obvious to me that this girl was an authentic artist." He was tempted to heap praise on her work, but fearing she might think him false, he put it simply: "In my opinion, no matter how difficult it is for you, you must continue to paint."

The girl asked him to come and see her other paintings, and she told him her name: Frida Kahlo. Where had Rivera heard that name before? Of course! This was the schoolgirl who had teased him back in 1922. Seeing recognition on Rivera's face, Kahlo quickly said, "Yes, so what? I was the girl in the auditorium, but that has absolutely nothing to do with now." So on the following Sunday, his next day off, Rivera knocked on the door of a blue house in a sleepy suburb called Coyoacán, where dogs and chickens wandered the streets. He spent the afternoon looking at Frida's paintings and savoring her delightful presence. "Frida had already become the most important fact in my life," he said.

Diego began coming often to the blue house. At other times, Frida sat with him while he painted. Soon, the two planned to marry, but the thought of having Diego Rivera as a son-in-law horrified Frida's parents. Rivera was divorced and a communist; and not only was he more than twice Frida's size, he was also, at forty-two, twice her age. "It was like a marriage between an elephant and a dove," they lamented. But then, Frida's father, Guillermo Kahlo, gave the matter some thought. He took Rivera aside. "Note well, my daughter is a sick person, and all her life she will be sick," he warned. Sick people run up medical bills, and Frida's would become her husband's to pay. "Think it over, and if you want to marry, I give my permission," Guillermo Kahlo said.

Rivera thought it over, and he did. The couple married on August 21, 1929, with the mayor of Coyoacán performing the service. The wedding "was celebrated in a very cordial atmosphere and with all modesty," according to the local newspaper. The bride wore a print dress, pearls, and a large *rebozo*, or shawl. The groom had traded his vast denim

DIEGO RIVERA, *THE NIGHTMARE OF WAR AND THE DREAM OF PEACE*, 1952.

Rivera works on a mural depicting a scene of war. He is painting Kahlo in the foreground, with children. Might she represent peace and hope for the future?

overalls for a suit and tie. When he posed with Frida for the wedding photograph, he held his mammoth Stetson hat at his side.

Rivera's artist friends liked to have a good time, and during the celebration that followed the ceremony, people drank too much tequila. At one point, the revelers danced their way up to a rooftop, where a woman's underwear had been hung out to dry. Lupe Marín even showed up. Rivera's ex-wife brazenly lifted Frida's skirt and announced to the crowd, "You see these two sticks? These are the legs Diego has now instead of mine!" When Diego pulled out a pistol and started shooting, Frida returned to her family in tears. Her husband showed up at the blue house several days later, finally ready to apologize, and took her home to begin their life together.

They married for love, but they soon discovered that love makes demands. It asked more of them than they were able to give. They found happiness together, but they also found heartache. Yet if there were times when they failed each other as human beings, they never did so as artists. Each respected the other's talent; each championed the other's work.

Each one also painted the other. Frida painted Diego as a giant of a man wearing brown shoes that were twenty times larger than her own. Diego painted Frida as a red-shirted communist handing out bayonets to an imagined workers' army.

Frida painted Diego as someone who was so much on her mind that his image bled through onto her forehead. He painted her as a face in a crowd.

They painted each other, and they painted themselves. Kahlo painted herself with flowers in her hair and wearing a necklace of thorns. She painted her body cracked open and studded with nails, because she lived in pain. She painted herself with monkeys, with parrots, and as a deer with arrows piercing its flesh. She painted her heavy eyebrows as the open wings of a swallow. Her greatest subject was herself. Frida Kahlo was "an artist who tore open her chest and heart to reveal the biological truth of her feelings," said Rivera.

Rivera painted himself as a young artist in a Spanish café, his face shadowed by a broad hat. He painted himself as an aging man with drooping eyelids, with gravity pulling his flesh toward the earth. But more often he looked outside of himself. He covered walls with expansive scenes of the present, past, or future. He filled every bit of space in these great murals with people, animals, plants, and machines. Diego Rivera was "the eternally curious one," said Frida Kahlo. "The whole of life continues to interest, to amaze him, with its changeability, and everything surprises him with its beauty."

2

THE CURIOUS ONE

················· ❁ ·················

*D*IEGO RIVERA was born in Guanajuato, a city pressed into a narrow valley northwest of Mexico City. A traveler from Baltimore who made his way to Guanajuato in 1889 called it a "quaint old mining town," and acknowledged its charm. A weary wanderer could rest on a stone bench shaded by palm trees in the Plaza de Mejía Mora, then Guanajuato's central park, and hear the soothing splash of fountains. Around the park, climbing flowers curled over the twisted railings of balconies and scented the air. Away from the central city, on Positos Street, the Riveras could peer through the highest windows of their house and look over rooftops to the green hills beyond.

Don Diego Rivera and his wife, María del Pilar, had tried three times to have a child. But each time the baby was stillborn. When María became pregnant again in 1886, the couple waited nervously. This pregnancy proceeded normally, though, and on December 8 it was time to summon Dr. Arizmendi. Later that day, María gave birth to twin boys. Yet she had lost so much blood that, try as he might, Dr. Arizmendi felt no pulse. With sadness he informed Don Diego that the babies lived but Doña María had died.

As Don Diego wept, the women in the household went to work. María's sister handed the infants to a wet nurse and prepared to dress the corpse. Then, as Doña María's longtime servant, Martha, kissed her dead mistress's forehead, she detected the faintest breath. Crying out, "She can hear me!" Martha brought the doctor back. He held a match to his patient's foot, and when it raised a blister, he confirmed what the old servant said. Doña María was alive, and she would recover.

The Riveras christened the twins Diego María and Carlos María. Both started life healthy, but while little Diego thrived, Carlos grew sickly. He died in 1888, only a year and a half old. His distraught mother mourned so deeply and so long that Dr. Arizmendi, desperate for some way to distract her, advised her to enter the university. Studying would draw her mind away from little Carlos's grave, he believed. For a woman to go to college was unusual in the 1800s, in Mexico or anywhere else, but María del Pilar followed her doctor's advice and enrolled in an obstetrics course. María, who had been a schoolteacher before marriage, wanted to help other mothers give birth.

A flock of women looked after little Diego. His mother, two aunts, the servant named Martha, and his Tarascan Indian nurse took turns fussing over him. When the family decided that fresh air would fatten him up and make him grow strong, his nurse took him to the mountains for a couple of years. Another female joined the family in 1891, when his sister, María, was born.

As soon as he was big enough, Diego sought the companionship of men. At Guanajuato's railroad station, he greeted the trainmen as comrades. He loved the mammoth steam-powered engines they drove and tended, and at home he drew pictures of them.

Twin brothers Carlos and Diego, when they were about a year old. Little Carlos had only a few more months to live.

Diego Rivera drew this picture of a train when he was a small boy. Big machines would remain one of the artist's favorite subjects.

Diego also listened closely as his father taught him to read. Don Diego Rivera was an educated man who worked for the state government. When he was younger he had tried to get rich mining silver in the hills around Guanajuato, but his mine yielded nothing of value. In 1884, Governor Manuel Gonzáles, a former president of Mexico, appointed him inspector of schools. A man with a strong social conscience, Don Diego also held a seat on the Guanajuato city council. He founded a school to train rural teach-ers, and he edited *El Demócrata*, the local liberal newspaper.

Don Diego was a freethinker who taught his little son to stay away from priests and to distrust the rituals of worship. Five-year-old Diego proved how well he had learned his lessons when Great-Aunt Vicenta secretly brought him to church, to teach him about the saints. Diego informed his old aunt that these saints were no more than statues carved from wood. Then, needing to set all the worshippers straight, he clambered onto the altar and denounced the notion that God sat on a cloud. Such a concept defied the laws of physics, he said. And, he added, anyone who gave money to the church was a fool. Soon an outraged priest came running. This child is a devil, he shouted, as Great-Aunt Vicenta grabbed Diego's hand and pulled him toward home.

A few months later, the Riveras left Guanajuato. Governor Gonzáles had died, and his appointees had fallen out of favor with the state's new leaders. On a winter day, María del Pilar lifted her children onto one of the trains Diego liked so much. They were headed for

Mexico City, their new home, less than a day's journey away. Don Diego joined them as soon as he finished his last school-inspection trip.

Built on the ruins of a great Aztec metropolis, Mexico's capital was home to roughly 345,000 people in 1892. Around him, Diego saw adults and children walking to work or school or church. Women with babies tied to their backs bought sweets and lottery tickets from street-side vendors. Tourists mingled with city residents at the flower market beside the cathedral, where sun-white lilies, buttery rosebuds, blood-red strawberries, and

From this street in Guanajuato people could look across the valley to the hillside beyond. This photograph is from the late 1800s, around the time of Rivera's birth.

glittering green parrots were offered for sale. The Riveras came to a city of wealth and need, where the rich bought luxuries in the dazzling shops on San Francisco Street and the poor crowded in one-room tenements without furniture or fresh air. The Riveras settled in a middle-class neighborhood, in a small house near the National Palace, the seat of government. Spaniards had built this imposing palace in 1693 with stones looted from Aztec temples.

While Don Diego worked as an inspector for the Department of Public Health, María del Pilar opened an obstetrical clinic. Diego attended a Catholic school—his mother's choice—but his parents sent him as well to evening classes at the San Carlos Academy, the nation's leading art school, because they saw that he had talent. Before long Diego's father took his education in hand and enrolled him in a military academy, but Diego balked so loudly at the academy's rigid rules that his stay there was short. He liked drawing battle scenes, but not soldiering.

By the time Diego was eleven, he had persuaded his parents to let him study at the San Carlos Academy full-time. He was younger than the other students, but he kept up with them as they mastered perspective and composition and sketched live models. One of his teachers, Santiago Rebull,

The poor were a common sight on the streets of Mexico City. The poverty he witnessed in Mexico and overseas influenced Diego Rivera to join the Communist Party.

singled Diego out for special instruction and praise. "These things which we call pictures and sketches are nothing but attempts to put onto a flat surface whatever is the essential in the movement of life," said the accomplished Mexican painter, who was then an old man. "My son, I do not know whether you will ever amount to anything. But you look carefully, and you have something in your head."

The teachers at the San Carlos Academy taught their students to paint portraits, landscapes, and biblical scenes in the realistic style of the European masters. Rebull himself painted religious subjects such as Christ on the cross and Abraham sacrificing his son, Isaac. Diego produced true-to-life pictures of trees, mountains, and houses. He made detailed sketches of human figures draped in cloth. He learned to scorn the bright colors of Mexico, the boldly painted figures and animals of its folk art, and the carvings left behind by the Aztecs and other civilizations that flourished in Mexico before the Spanish arrived in the 1500s.

Yet he discovered another kind of art on his walks to and from school. He stood often in front of the print shop where José Guadalupe Posada produced posters, covers for sheet music, and illustrations for newspapers. In Posada's window hung his pictures of popular singers, rail accidents, bandits robbing victims at gunpoint, and the decorated, dressed-up skeletons of Mexican folk celebrations. His prints enriched the lives of thousands of Mexicans who knew nothing about European painting.

Diego Rivera graduated with honors from the San Carlos Academy in 1906. He was nineteen years old and had grown tall. He had large, heavy-lidded brown eyes, and he brushed his dark hair back from his face. Twenty-six of his pictures hung in the show of graduating students' work, where they attracted the attention of art critics and government officials. One person who viewed the show was Teodoro Dehesa, governor of the state of Veracruz, which borders the Gulf of Mexico. Dehesa, an art lover, was so impressed with Diego's work that he provided funds for this talented youth to get further training, in Europe. Diego excitedly made plans to sail at the end of the year; meanwhile, he had six months to spend in Mexico, sketching, painting, and having fun.

Rivera had a daring imagination. In later years he liked to shock listeners by claiming

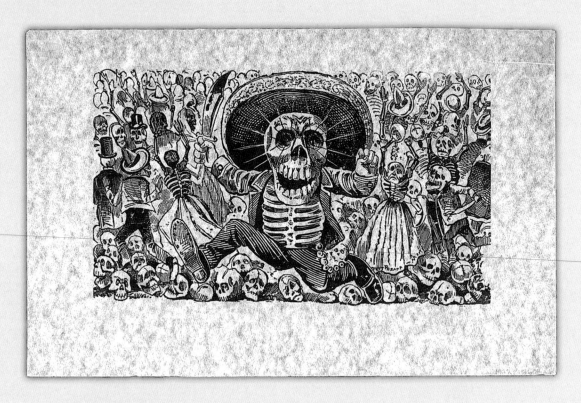

This print by the popular artist José Guadalupe Posada shows a fiendish skeletal figure waving his sword while behind him a skeleton population raises arms in fear.

that during these months he tasted human flesh. "Best of all," he said, were "women's brains in vinaigrette." The truth was much tamer, however. Rivera made friends with a group of artists and intellectuals who published a journal called *Savia Moderna*. In its pages they spoke out against art as it was taught at the San Carlos Academy, which to them reflected the restrictive policies of Mexico's president, Porfirio Díaz. An old man with a chest full of military medals, Díaz ruled Mexico like a dictator. He censored the press and controlled the courts. He had built up the Mexican economy, but he had done so by letting foreign investors buy Mexican factories, farms, and mineral rights. Diego's new friends wanted art to be free and to portray the dreams and emotions of the human spirit.

One painter went further and called for Mexican artists to create art that was truly

Mexican. He was Gerardo Murillo, but he called himself Dr. Atl, a name he derived from the Aztec word for water. Dr. Atl had walked the length and breadth of Mexico to study its ancient ruins and bathe in its rivers. He had sketched along the way, amassing a great pile of drawings, but he is remembered best for his many paintings of Mexico's volcanoes. He depicted them rising above clouds, spewing smoke, or resting dormant under fantastical skies.

Dr. Atl had also traveled throughout Europe, and he often talked to younger artists about the wondrous art he had seen there. He told them of the French Impressionists, who were experimenting with color and capturing the effects of light. With his sharp eyes peering out from under a strong brow, he praised the glorious murals of the Italian Renaissance. "The great mural painters!" he would exclaim. "The immense Renaissance frescoes, as incredible and mysterious as the Pharaohs' pyramids." The muralists had painted on fresh, wet plaster, which absorbed pigment as it dried. In this way, a painting became a permanent part of a wall or ceiling. The name for this kind of mural, fresco, comes from the Italian word *fresco*, meaning "fresh." The old Italian frescoes were mysterious, Dr. Atl said, because the techniques used to create them had been lost for four hundred years. If only Mexican artists could paint such wonders in an authentically Mexican way!

Diego Rivera listened to these new and stimulating ideas. When the six months were up, he left Mexico and sailed for Europe, reaching Spain in January 1907. He journeyed inland to Madrid, where the sun shone brightly nearly every day and the sky was deep blue. Carrying a letter of introduction from Dr. Atl, he presented himself at the studio of Eduardo Chicharro, a popular artist, and asked to be taken on as a student. Chicharro was a superb craftsman whose work had earned him many medals. He loved to paint the female form, either nude or in the costume of a foreign land or an exotic region of Spain. He had much to teach his student about achieving fine details and sumptuous color effects.

As he finished canvases, Rivera shipped them to Governor Dehesa in Veracruz as proof that he was learning. Chicharro also sent reports to Dehesa, assuring him that the state's money was being well spent. Rivera was making "astonishing progress," he wrote; the young man was a "tireless worker."

How true this was! If Rivera set up his easel first thing in the morning, he would still be painting when the sun went down. He was living in a hotel near the Prado, Madrid's great art museum. He could often be found there, copying masterpieces by Velázquez, Goya, and other great Spanish artists. He painted outdoors as well, especially when Chicharro took him to see new places. They visited Salamanca, a city with narrow streets, which since 1218 had been the site of a university, and Ávila, a town enclosed by a medieval stone wall. They toured the Basque Country, near the French border, and in May 1907 they traveled to beautiful Barcelona, on the Mediterranean Sea.

Back home in Mexico City, María del Pilar worried that her son was lonely and needed looking after. She wrote to Diego to say that she and his sister, María, were coming to Spain to take care of him.

Oh, no! Diego was twenty years old and living on his own for the first time. The last thing he wanted was to have his mother there, watching his every move. María del Pilar had

DIEGO RIVERA, *MADAME FISHER*, 1918

Rivera drew this pencil portrait in his early, realistic style.

grown hard to please and quick to erupt in tears or anger. She acted impulsively, without thinking through the consequences of her deeds. What could Diego do? He sent a letter to his father, tactfully suggesting that his mother wait a year. Then, when she came, he would escort her to Paris and Rome. He received a response—not from his father but from his hurt, angry mother. Diego need not worry, María del Pilar wrote. He would never have to see his mother again. Unruffled, Diego wrote once more to his father to explain that he spent all his time working and was too busy for guests.

In 1975, Mexico commemorated the hundredth anniversary of the birth of Gerardo Murillo, the artist known as Dr. Atl, with a postage stamp.

Diego was making friends among the young artists of Madrid. One was the painter María Blanchard, who was born in Spain in 1881. Blanchard stood less than five feet tall, because her spine had been badly curved since infancy. Rivera admired her fine mind as well as her beautiful hands. "María was cultured, and she penetrated into the soul of the things in this life," said the Spanish painter Francisco Pompey, who also looked up to Blanchard.

In 1908, Blanchard left Madrid to study in Paris. The following year, Rivera, too, felt the urge to move on. He longed to see so many places, and so much art. In the spring he said goodbye to his teacher and took a train to Paris, where he found a room in the Hôtel de Suez, a place popular with Spanish-speaking students. The hotel's tall windows offered a view of Notre Dame de Paris, the city's magnificent cathedral. He set up his easel alongside the River Seine or in the galleries of the Louvre, the renowned museum of art. He saw nothing of María Blanchard, who had never tried to contact the other Spanish art students in Paris.

Rivera next went to Belgium with another Mexican painter, Enrique Friedmann. One evening, in the Belgian city of Bruges, the two walked into a café to get something to eat and saw two women sitting there. One was Rivera's friend María Blanchard, who introduced the men to her companion, Angelina Beloff. The fair, blue-eyed Beloff had studied art in Russia, where she was born. In 1909, after her parents died, she took her inheritance and moved to Paris, and there she met Blanchard. The four artists began spending their days together, sketching and painting the landscape around Bruges. Beloff painted the city's canals, and Rivera and Blanchard captured the lights of Bruges at night. Beloff spoke no Spanish, and Rivera knew no Russian or French, which Beloff spoke well. Even though they managed to communicate in English, she had no idea what he was saying when he told her he was falling in love. She finally understood when he gave her a charcoal drawing with the dedication "To Mademoiselle Angelina Beloff as a souvenir of my affection."

Picturesque canals flow through the Belgian city of Bruges.

From Bruges, the friends took a boat to London. Rivera was eager to see paintings by Hogarth, Turner, and other great English artists of the past. What made a deeper impression on him than the art hanging in the British Museum, however, was the terrible poverty he saw. For a century London had been a center of economic growth, but its prosperity had come at the expense of its laborers. Factories and sweatshops paid wages that barely kept people afloat. Old age, illness, a wage earner's death—any setback could sink a family into poverty. Everywhere in London, it seemed, there were hungry people rooting through trash cans for food, homeless beggars sleeping under archways, and children working as prostitutes to survive. Rivera never would forget these distressing sights. They would cause him to think hard about how societies should share their wealth.

The artists made their way back to Paris. Friedmann drifted away from the others, but Rivera and Beloff grew closer. Rivera wrote letters to her, and to Blanchard, too, when he sailed home to Mexico in October 1910 for a show of his paintings. He addressed Angelina as "my beloved wife, my angel," although they had not married.

An unknown beginner in Europe, Diego Rivera had become a celebrity at home. Newspapers printed pictures of him sporting the beard he had grown and called him "a very great artist." One art critic praised his exhibition as "an artistic spectacle, worthy to see and admire, because it gives evidence of the progress that Mexican painters have made." The exhibition was part of a grand celebration marking one hundred years from the start of Mexico's war for independence from Spain. The show opened on November 20 and was such a big success that the closing date was postponed from December 11 to December 20, to let more people see it. Thirteen of the thirty-five paintings on display found buyers. Even Mexico's first lady, Doña Carmen Romero Rubio de Díaz, bought a picture, of a Basque fisherman and his wife.

President Díaz's years in office were soon to end. In the 1910 election, he ran against Francisco Madero, a wealthy rancher who was popular with the people. Díaz made sure Madero lost the race by having him arrested for a time and then rigging the vote. Refusing to accept this phony defeat, Madero stole away to the United States, and from there he led

Peasants stream across the land, fleeing the bloodshed and destruction of the Mexican Revolution. They will seek shelter and safety in a refugee camp.

an armed attack on Casas Grandes, a town in the northern Mexican state of Chihuahua, in February 1911. This one assault was like a tiny spark landing on a parched field that was waiting to ignite. To people throughout Mexico who were desperate to reclaim their rights and their land, Madero's attack was a signal to act. Peasants took up arms under renegade leaders such as Pancho Villa and Emiliano Zapata. By April the fighting had spread to eighteen states, and the Mexican Revolution was well under way.

When he was a famous artist, Rivera liked to claim that in 1910 he had been plotting to assassinate President Díaz, but in truth he only followed news reports of the violence and unrest. After his show closed, he took a train out into the country to paint. "I could not remain in the city and was unwilling to return to you without even two or three things to show you," he explained to Angelina Beloff. He completed two large landscapes, and he was back in Paris before the Mexican government signed a treaty with the rebel forces on May 21, 1911.

President Díaz was forced to resign. Ten days later, he was in Veracruz, ready to board the steamship that would carry him to exile in Europe. With tears in his eyes, he told the crowd that had gathered to see him off, "If the Fatherland should ever want my services, then solemnly I undertake, as a gentleman and a soldier, to be always at the soldiers' side and beneath their flag, so that I may defend the cherished soil of Mexico, until I have poured out my last drop of blood." These were ardent words, but he was never to return. And despite the treaty, fighting and political unrest would continue in Mexico for nine more years.

3

An Accidental Artist

❀

DIEGO RIVERA was already grown up and far away in Madrid studying painting when Frida Kahlo was born. Kahlo claimed she was born in the momentous year of revolution, 1910, but she really entered the world three years earlier, on July 6, 1907. She was the third of four girls born to Guillermo Kahlo and his second wife, Matilde Calderón.

Guillermo Kahlo had built the family's home, the blue house on a street corner in Coyoacán, to be a cheerful place. Sunlight flowed in through its tall windows, and each room opened onto a central courtyard. There were no hallways, so the family walked from room to room to get to a different part of the house, or they took a shortcut across the courtyard.

Frida's father had been born in Germany, to a Hungarian Jewish family. His parents had called him Wilhelm, but after he grew up and moved to Mexico in the 1890s, he adopted the Spanish version of his name, Guillermo. He was a widower with two young daughters when he fell in love with Matilde Calderón, the petite young woman who worked beside him in a jewelry store. The couple married, although Matilde was a Roman Catholic and deeply religious and Guillermo claimed to be an atheist. Matilde's father, a photographer, taught his son-in-law to take pictures. By the time Frida was born, Guillermo Kahlo was working for the government, photographing Mexico's historic architecture.

Matilde Calderón was dainty and pretty, "like a little bell," Frida said. "When she went to market, she gracefully cinched her waist and carried her basket coquettishly." Matilde taught her girls to sew clothing and do fine embroidery. She took them to Mass and tried to raise them as good Catholics, but Frida and her younger sister, Cristina, rejected the church's teachings.

Guillermo Kahlo's daughters from his first marriage grew up in a convent, raised by nuns. Even without them, a big family lived in the blue house, so something was always happening there. When Frida's sister Matilde turned fifteen, she ran off with her boyfriend and got married. Frida, who was still a little girl, helped Matilde sneak out a balcony window. The girls' mother was furious when she learned what had happened. She refused to forgive her oldest daughter for being so reckless or to let her come back home, and she stayed angry about the elopement for twelve years.

Matilde Calderón and Guillermo Kahlo were photographed on their wedding day.

Frida became the focus of concern when she was six years old and came down with polio. Before the 1950s, when vaccines first offered protection, people lived in terror of this viral illness. Polio can damage the nervous system, causing lasting disability, paralysis, and even death. If polio struck, families could only make a patient comfortable and hope for the best. Frida spent nine lonely months in her room. She escaped through play, by breathing a vapory film on the window and tracing a door in it with her finger. Waiting on the other side was her imaginary friend, a girl her own age who laughed and danced and listened to Frida's worries. Meanwhile, Frida's anxious parents bathed her tender right leg in water scented with walnuts, and slowly she recovered.

When Frida's doctor prescribed exercise to strengthen her leg, Guillermo took the advice to heart. Few Mexican girls took part in sports, but Frida's father made sure that she swam, played soccer, wrestled, and climbed trees. "My toys were those of a boy: skates, bicycles," Frida said. Her right leg remained shorter and thinner than her left one, though, and the other children teased her. When they called her *pata de palo* (peg leg), she shouted curses back.

Guillermo thought Frida was the smartest of his daughters and the one most like him. He gave her books to read and taught her about insects and plants. He took her to the studio above the jewelry store where he once worked, and there he showed her how he made photographs in the darkroom. He taught her to add color to black-and-white prints by brushing on weak solutions of paints or dyes. Her school bag was always jammed full of natural specimens, photographs, and books.

In 1922, when Frida was fifteen, her father enrolled her in the National Preparatory School, the finest high school in Mexico City. Two thousand students attended this school, but only thirty-five were girls. Boys and girls alike took tough classes in mathematics, the sciences, and foreign languages to prepare them for college. Frida liked biology and hoped to become a doctor.

Before long, she fell in with a group of friends. These boys and girls called themselves the Cachuchas, meaning "Caps," after the school caps that students had to wear. The Cachuchas were known for being brainy, because they liked to discuss books and poetry, but they were also renowned for their pranks. It was the Cachuchas who brought a donkey to school and rode it up and down the halls. It was the Cachuchas who lit a firecracker during a lecture, and who stifled their laughs when the professor droned on through the explosion as if nothing had happened. It was the Cachuchas, and especially Frida, who tormented Diego Rivera when he came to paint a mural in the school's auditorium.

A street in sleepy Coyoacán, as it looked at the close of the nineteenth century.

Frida "had a fresh, perhaps ingenuous and childlike manner, but at the same time she was quick and dramatic in her urge to discover life," recalled Alejandro Gómez Arias, the leader of the Cachuchas, who was Frida's boyfriend.

Alejandro was with Frida in Mexico City on the gray afternoon of September 17, 1925. Heading home, the two hopped onto a crowded wooden bus and made their way to the back, where they found seats together. The bus had reached the San Juan Market, where vendors offered the freshest bounty of the land and sea, when the passengers saw a streetcar approaching from the side. The streetcar moved steadily forward, and soon it was pushing hard against the bus. The side of the bus bowed inward and shattered, sending people, parcels, and shards of wood flying in all directions.

Alejandro landed under the streetcar and escaped serious injury, but Frida was far less lucky. The force of the collision pushed a metal handrail straight through her pelvis, the way a matador's sword pierces a bull, Frida said. She suffered grave internal injuries, and her skeleton was as broken as the bus. Her right leg, the one weakened by polio, was fractured in eleven places, and her right foot was crushed. Alejandro saw that Frida's clothes had been ripped away. A packet of golden powder that someone was carrying had torn open, and this dust had fallen onto Frida's bleeding body like sparkling snow. An ambulance carried Frida to the nearest hospital, where surgeons repaired the worst damage and marveled that she had survived.

Frida was ten when a photographer snapped this picture of the Kahlo sisters. Adriana stands behind Cristina and Matilde; Frida stands to the right.

Frida's father grew ill when news of the accident reached Coyoacán, and her sister Adriana, a new bride, fainted away. "Just imagine, my poor little mother says she cried like a madwoman for three days," Frida wrote to Alejandro, once she was well enough to hold a pen. It upset Frida's parents to see her lying in a hospital bed with her body encased in plaster casts, so they seldom visited. It was Matilde, her outcast sister, who came every day and raised Frida's spirits with conversation and jokes. Frida bore up well during the day, but in the dark she felt most alone. "In this hospital death dances around my bed at night," she wrote.

After spending weeks in the hospital, Frida convalesced at home. Her body was so damaged that she would live in pain for the rest of her life. Again and again in the coming years, doctors would operate on her spine or fit her with a plaster corset to hold her bones in place. She missed her final exams that fall, and she was too ill to register for spring classes. She gave up her dream of being a doctor.

Bored and needing something to do, she borrowed some paints and brushes from her father and started to make pictures. Matilde Calderón hired a carpenter to build an easel that would let Frida paint while lying down, because the doctors had warned that sitting up would place too much pressure on her still-mending spine. Frida was too fragile to go out and paint landscapes and city scenes, as many artists do. She painted the subjects available to her, her sisters Adriana and Cristina, and friends from school and the neighborhood who visited. When no callers came, she looked in a mirror to paint the one subject who remained: herself. The women and girls who appear in these early portraits, including Frida, appear long and slender, with gracefully posed hands. Frida painted them against imaginary backgrounds of dark waves, fanciful trees, starry skies, and clouds. The schoolgirl who had planned to study medicine was born anew as an artist. Unlike Diego Rivera, who spent years working with living masters, Frida Kahlo learned to paint all by herself.

She sent her first self-portrait to Alejandro as a gift, hoping it would help him remember her. But her loneliness worsened when he left to spend four months in Europe, studying German and traveling. She wrote him long letters in which she promised to be better soon, but the romance was over. When Alejandro returned to Mexico, he started college and found a new girlfriend. He still cared for Frida, but life was leading him into the world and away from the invalid in Coyoacán.

While Frida Kahlo lay in bed and stared in a mirror, studying the contours of her cheeks and the curve of her heavy eyebrows, Diego Rivera was not far away. Having left Paris and returned to his homeland, he was painting murals in the chapel of the Natural Agricultural School at Chapingo, just outside Mexico City. The chapel was no longer used for worship. Beginning in 1924, President Plutarco Elías Calles had closed Roman Catholic monasteries, convents, schools, and chapels throughout the country. The move was part of a long power struggle between the Mexican government and the church to which many Mexicans belonged. Under Calles, Mexico made it a crime for priests to wear clerical robes in public or criticize the nation's leaders. Priests also had to register with the government. So far, Mexican Catholics had responded nonviolently. They boycotted government-operated public services, such as buses; Catholic teachers resigned from their jobs at public schools. In July 1926 the church suspended religious services, hoping to rouse the faithful in further peaceful protest against the new laws. Whether the situation would remain peaceful was anyone's guess. "The hour is approaching for the decisive battle," warned President Calles.

Rivera, a nonbeliever, covered the chapel walls with scenes of peasants working the land. At the front, where the altar once stood, he painted a great nude, a goddess of the earth. Rivera's art had changed since 1911, when he was still painting like a European. His murals at Chapingo feature Mexican subjects, and his painting style pays tribute to the folk art of his native land and the carvings of its ancient people. On the chapel ceiling he painted a red star, and over it the hands of workers holding a hammer and scythe—the communist symbols. From this time on, his work would often feature communist themes.

Rivera had joined the Mexican Communist Party in the fall of 1922. The party had been founded in 1919, in the wake of the Russian Revolution, which had transformed tsarist Russia into the Union of Soviet Socialist Republics, the world's first communist state. The concept at the heart of communism—that all people share equally in a nation's wealth—began to attract followers decades earlier, in 1848. In that year Karl Marx and Friedrich Engels published the *Communist Manifesto*. The two German philosophers presented history as a continuous class struggle, with the working class trying to rise up and better themselves, and the wealthier class holding the workers down. The *Communist Manifesto* and another book, *Das Kapital,* which Marx published in 1867, blamed slums and poverty on the capitalist system, which enabled the wealthy to exploit the working class for their own gain. Marx and Engels also traced economic depressions and the suffering they caused to the volatile workings of capitalism.

Communism attracted idealists in Mexico and other countries. It certainly appealed to Rivera, who recalled vividly the poverty he had seen in Mexico City and London. The Mexican Communist Party organized bakers, railroad workers, miners, and other laborers into unions. The artists within the party formed an organization of their own, the Union of Technical Workers, Painters, and Sculptors.

The communists dreamed of a day when farms and factories belonged to everyone. When that day came, peasants would receive the same share of food and manufactured goods as the landowners and bosses who had grown rich on their labor. Under communism, every family would live in a decent house, and every child would learn in a good school. Poverty and wealth would be relics of the past, or so Rivera and his fellow communists believed. It was a beautiful idea.

4

REBORN

*B*ACK IN 1911, Rivera and Angelina Beloff had exchanged vows of love and loyalty, although they never married. They lived together in the section of Paris called Montparnasse, which was a center of artistic life. In September 1912, Diego and Angelina moved into a run-down building at 26, rue du Départ, near the Montparnasse railroad station. The whistles and rumbles of trains never ceased, and smoke from their engines dirtied the air, but Diego hardly minded. He loved trains and machinery as much as he had in childhood.

He displayed his landscapes and portraits in exhibitions held by the Society of Independent Artists. For anyone wanting to see the newest happenings in the art world, these shows were the place to be. In 1913, all of Paris was talking about the work of the Cubists. Pablo Picasso, Georges Braque, and other daring artists were painting objects and people from different angles all at once, all on the same flat canvas. Some people looked at these paintings and saw beauty, others saw only shapes, and neither group was wrong. "Subject-matter now counts for little or nothing at all," explained the French writer Guillaume Apollinaire. "The artist sacrifices everything to the truths and imperatives of a higher nature."

To Diego Rivera, Cubism offered fresh ideas. He saw that the Cubists had freed artists from any need to paint realistically. "Everything about the movement fascinated and intrigued me. It was a revolutionary movement, questioning everything that had previously been said and done in art," he said. "Cubism broke down forms as they had been seen for centuries and was creating out of the fragments new forms and, ultimately, new worlds." He began to produce Cubist works of his own: portraits of Angelina and others, a painting of the Eiffel Tower, and still-life arrangements.

Rivera met Picasso in the cold first months of 1914. Born in Spain in 1881, Picasso was already recognized as a leading modern artist. He invited Rivera to his studio to see his newest work, and he visited the rue du Départ to see what Rivera was doing. "Will and energy blazed from his round, black eyes," Rivera observed. "His black, glossy hair was cut short like the hair of a circus strongman." An open-hearted man who loved human contact, Picasso sat with Rivera on a shabby sofa in the rooms near the railroad station and talked about art.

Rivera and Angelina Beloff pose between two other couples, some of their Paris friends.

In April 1914, a Paris gallery hosted a show of Rivera's Cubist paintings. Art collectors were eager to acquire Cubist works, and most of the paintings sold. This was fortunate for Rivera, because he had lost his government support in 1913. In the summer he and Angelina Beloff went to Spain to hike and sketch. They stayed with María Blanchard and other artists on the serene, mountainous island of Majorca, where farmers raised grapes and grain. Off in the countryside, away from newspapers, they lived contentedly out of touch with the rest of the world. In mid-July they learned of an incident that people from Europe to Mexico and beyond had been talking about for weeks. On June 28, a Serbian

DIEGO RIVERA, *MARINO ALMORZANDO* (*SAILOR AT LUNCH*), 1914.

*An abstract painting of a sailor, one of Rivera's
Cubist works.*

assassin had shot and killed Archduke Franz Ferdinand, the heir to the throne of Austria-Hungary.

The shooting brought simmering ethnic feuds to the boiling point. On July 28 Austria-Hungary declared war on Serbia. Next, Russia entered the war on the Serbian side. Then Germany declared war on Russia, Belgium, and France. World War I had begun.

As for Rivera, Beloff, and their friends, "[We felt] as remote from the conflict on the continent as if we were in the South Seas," Rivera said. They saw some effects of the war on society when they went back to Paris in 1915. They quickly learned that the market for paintings had dried up; the once popular art shows had been canceled, and galleries had closed. Many artists had gone off to fight on the side of France. Rivera later claimed that he tried to enlist in the French army but that military doctors had declared him unfit. Whether or not this is true, he and Beloff and the other artists who remained in Paris were often broke, hungry, and cold.

Paris grew quiet. A fuel shortage kept cars off the city streets. The noisy dance halls shut down and reopened as soup kitchens. City leaders canceled festivals and public celebrations, saying it was wrong to make merry while their countrymen were dying in battle.

One sound alone broke the silence: the terrifying booms of the big German guns that were bombarding the city.

The busiest places in Paris were the railroad stations. Trains pulled out carrying new recruits to the battlefront. Other trains returned from the front with soldiers whose bodies had been wounded by bullets and whose minds had been scarred by the brutality they had seen. Refugees poured into Paris from Belgium and northern France, where the fighting was heavy. At the same time, people who could afford to leave town boarded trains for the relative safety that could be found to the south.

Bombed-out buildings like this print shop were a common sight in Paris during World War I.

In the midst of this hardship and distress, Diego's mother and sister showed up. María del Pilar had fought with her husband and left him. Her earlier anger at her son forgotten, she made her way with her daughter to Paris. She planned to open a maternity clinic in Madrid, but after reaching Europe she learned that Spain had a law against foreigners practicing obstetrics. The two women saw that staying with Diego would be impossible; he was too poor to support four people. Diego's sister contacted their father, who arranged for his high-strung wife and his daughter to go home.

Soon after they left, Angelina became pregnant. On August 11, 1916, she gave birth to a boy, who was christened Diego María, after his father. He was a healthy baby during his first, warm months, but then winter came. All of Paris struggled in the cold, but young children suffered most. When he was fourteen months old, Dieguito—Little Diego—died of pneumonia. Angelina nursed her failing child alone, because Diego was absent during his son's final days. He was dividing his time between Angelina and another woman, Marevna Vorobëv, a Cubist painter from Russia. In truth, Dieguito's illness was too much for him to bear. When he learned of the little boy's death, he collapsed.

Happiness returned a year later, when the long war ended. A defeated Germany signed a peace agreement on November 11, 1918. As news of the armistice reached Paris, people poured out of buildings and into the city's boulevards and parks. Crowds paraded arm in arm, singing "La Marseillaise," the French national anthem. *"Le jour de gloire est arrivé,"* they sang: The day of glory has arrived! Women showered soldiers with flowers and kisses. Children climbed onto statues to watch the city-wide party that lasted well into the night.

When his lover Marevna gave birth to a daughter, Marika, in 1919, Diego refused to acknowledge her as his child. He called Marika a "daughter of the Armistice," implying that she was conceived during the great celebration that erupted in Paris at the end of World War I, and that any man might be her father. Marevna called him a coward and hoped he would have a change of heart.

Instead he changed his mind about art and abandoned Cubism. He wanted to paint in his own style, not the Cubists', but he had yet to figure out what his style should be.

He explained his dilemma to his new friend Élie Faure. A doctor who treated wounded soldiers during the war, Faure was also an expert in art history. He believed that progress in art followed a cycle, and that ways of painting in bygone eras were bound to gain importance again. To Faure, painting in Italy was "the most important phenomenon in the history of Europe between the twelfth and sixteenth centuries." According to Faure, Western civilization owed just about everything to Italian painting. Not only had it "laid the foundations of the modern spirit," but it had also "made possible, in fact, the rise of the individual and of science." He urged Rivera to go to Italy and study the murals painted by Leonardo da Vinci, Michelangelo, and other Renaissance masters—the same murals that had awed Dr. Atl.

Sometime in 1920, Rivera packed up his paints, brushes, and sketchpad and went to Italy. He asked for and received funds from the Mexican government for this trip, after agreeing to return to Mexico and paint murals in public buildings. He visited Milan, Florence, Padua, and Rome. In cathedrals and chapels, he saw walls and ceilings adorned with wondrous murals depicting Christian subjects: the Virgin and the Christ child; the Last Supper; the Crucifixion. He saw frightening scenes of damned souls being cast into hell. The murals were full of detail and peopled with saints, angels, and ordinary mortals.

Rivera sketched furiously, producing more than three hundred drawings of the magnificent art he saw. In Florence he also sketched the scaffolding modern Italian artists used to paint high above the floor. He wanted to be sure that Mexican carpenters could build the same kind of scaffolding for him when he went home. Returning briefly to Paris, Rivera said separate goodbyes to Angelina and Marevna. He told each woman that he would send her money to join him in Mexico, but these were empty promises. In July 1921, he sailed out of their lives. Marevna wrote years later, "I still hoped in my heart of hearts that one day everything would turn out for the best. . . . When a love affair is over, there is nothing to be done about that; but when one leaves children behind one, it is one's duty to think of their destiny."

Rivera thought only of his future. Having been gone for a decade, he had forgotten the beauty of the Mexican landscape. "All the colors I saw appeared to be heightened; they were clearer, richer, finer, and more full of light," he wrote. Suddenly, the whole country and its history waited to be painted. Rivera declared, "I am reborn."

The Mexican art world had changed in the ten years Diego Rivera was away. The revolution had reminded people how much they loved their country; it had made them proud to trace their history back to the centuries before Christopher Columbus reached the New World. An exhibition of art from this pre-Columbian time, organized by Dr. Atl, rekindled interest in the nation's culture. This new enthusiasm gave rise to an artistic trend. It was called *Mexicanidad,* meaning "Mexicanness." Artists of the Mexicanidad movement wanted to paint like Mexicans rather than Europeans.

Dr. Atl had also formed the Centro Artístico (Artistic Center), which arranged for murals to be painted in public buildings. He assigned Rivera to paint one in the auditorium of the National Preparatory School, while he painted a mural of his own—of a volcano, of course—in another part of the building. Painting murals was different from painting on canvas, so Rivera had a great deal to learn and discover as he went along. He had to get used to working high above the floor on scaffolding, and to apply pigments quickly, before the wet plaster that had been smoothed onto a wall grew too dry to soak up his colors. As a twentieth-century artist, he tried to replicate the forgotten methods of the Renaissance using modern materials.

Excitement about murals was spreading. The new secretary of education, José Vasconcelos, was commissioning Mexican artists to paint them in government agencies. Vasconcelos called on artists to paint fresh subjects, to be inventive, and to strive for greatness. His aim, he said, "was to put the public in contact with great artists rather than with mediocrities." The new murals had their critics, but Mexico soon became known throughout the world as the leading country for mural painting. Artists came from the United States, France, and Japan to work and study there.

Rivera would emerge as one of three great Mexican muralists. The second was David Alfaro Siqueiros, another ardent communist, whose style was more abstract than Rivera's.

Siqueiros's murals depicting the struggles of ordinary people are full of movement and bold shapes.

The third muralist, José Clemente Orozco, was the most pessimistic. He painted in earthy browns, deep reds, and black. Like Kahlo, he had survived an accident in his teenage years. While playing with gunpowder, he had set off an explosion that mangled his hands so badly that the left one had to be amputated. The blast had also damaged his hearing and vision.

It was Secretary Vasconcelos who hired Diego Rivera to paint the walls of the Ministry of Education, and Rivera was thankful for the income. He had arrived home to find his father ill with cancer and no longer able to work. In late 1921, he sent

José Clemente Orozco chose dark colors—browns, reds, and black—to set the mood in his paintings.

a letter to Marevna informing her that his father was dead. The artist mourned the man who had been his first teacher and who had encouraged him to succeed. In his letter Rivera mentioned little Marika, who had been ill. "Perhaps he thought that she was going to die too," Marevna guessed. She noted, "It was in this letter that he told me of his new passion for Lupe Marín and I realized that he would forsake my child and me for this woman." Marevna's intuition was right. By the time his mother died, in 1923, Rivera indeed had a wife. He had married tall, green-eyed Guadalupe Marín in June 1922. Marevna heard nothing more from him.

"Lupe was a beautiful, spirited animal," in Rivera's words, with the snarling lips of a tiger and the strong legs of a young horse. She modeled for many of the female figures in

Rivera's work, including the great nude in the chapel at Chapingo. She and Diego lived on one of the upper floors of an apartment house near the Zócalo, the grand square at the heart of Mexico City, in a section that was old and shabby but still beautiful. From their windows they looked out on the rooftops of other buildings, where people hung laundry and kept rabbits, chickens, and fighting cocks. Lupe and Diego would have two daughters: Guadalupe, born in 1924, and Ruth, born in 1927.

As a Communist Party member, Rivera marched in parades and spoke at rallies in support of labor unions and the working class. He helped publish *El Machete*, the party newspaper. Costing just a few centavos per issue, *El Machete* spread communist ideas to peasants and laborers. Poet and party member Graciela Amador wrote that the paper was intended to aid humanity, like the broad knife for which it was named:

Communists demonstrate outside the United States Embassy in Mexico on May 1, 1929.

> To open paths in shadowed
>   woods,
> To decapitate serpents, to cut
>   down weeds,
> And to humble the pride of
>   the impious rich.

Rivera served the party well. In 1923 he was elected to its governing body, the Central Committee.

Comrades march through Moscow carrying banners and flags. Rivera painted this scene when he visited the Soviet Union in 1927 and 1928.

Diego Rivera—muralist, communist, lover of women—was also becoming a tourist attraction. High on a scaffold, wearing his big Stetson hat and sporting a pistol in a holster, he entertained visitors with fantastic, made-up tales of his life's adventures—how he had fought in the Russian Revolution, for example. "Where could one meet a jollier, heartier giant than Rivera?" remarked Witter Bynner, a writer from the United States who went to see Rivera paint. "And what a joy to watch the workmanship of his big hands." (It is interesting that Bynner called Rivera's hands big, whereas Marevna Vorobëv and others thought they looked small.)

When Ralph Stackpole, a sculptor from San Francisco, met Rivera and saw his murals, he decided to bring this artist to his home city one day. Traveling with Stackpole was his friend Leo Eloesser, a well-respected physician. Like other visitors, Eloesser delighted in Rivera's larger-than-life imagination. "He regaled me during several days with his experiences in the Boer War in South Africa, a country in which I am sure he never set foot," Eloesser later recalled.

The observant doctor wrote down his impressions of Rivera as he painted, noting that "he worked on the walls with infinite care, slowly, precisely, with small brush strokes." Like others, Eloesser commented on Rivera's stamina: "I have seen him spend twenty-four and thirty-six hours and more on the scaffolding when he wanted to complete a stint; not sleeping, eating maybe a few tortillas or taking a cup of chocolate that was brought to him."

Another spectator was Italian-born Tina Modotti, who came to Mexico with the American photographer Edward Weston. Modotti was one of Weston's models and a photographer in her own right. Men found her attractive, and she had many lovers. Rivera invited her to take pictures of his work at the Ministry of Education. The professional relationship grew into an affair that lasted several months and ended the marriage of Diego Rivera and Lupe Marín.

In 1927, Rivera traveled to the Soviet Union as part of a Mexican delegation for the celebrations marking the tenth anniversary of the Russian Revolution. When he returned, he encountered another woman, one who was to have a stronger hold on his heart than Lupe, Angelina, or any of the others ever could. Frida Kahlo entered his life.

5

SOUTH AND NORTH OF THE BORDER LINE

❀

*N*EWLY MARRIED, Frida and Diego lived at a stylish address, 140 Paseo de la Reforma. Their dining room furniture had been passed along by a friend, and their yellow kitchen table was a gift from Frida's mother. Even with help from a maid, Frida struggled to be mistress of her own home. She had never kept house before, and the Communist Party had sent four other people to live briefly with the couple. If Diego got sick, which happened soon after the wedding, he expected Frida to consult the doctor and give him his medicine.

Help came from Lupe Marín, who took Frida shopping and helped her pick out pots and pans. Then Diego's ex-wife taught his new wife how to cook. Many days, Frida packed Diego's lunch in a basket and carried it to where he was working; then she sat near him on the scaffolding while he painted. He had started a series of murals in the National Palace, the seat of government that was near his childhood home. It was a huge project, one that Rivera would leave and return to for the rest of his career. When complete, these murals would present Mexico from the time before Spanish conquest through the 1920s and beyond. Rivera still put in long days, because he was not only painting murals. In April 1929, he had been made director of the San Carlos Academy, where he had studied art as a boy.

There he had everyone working as hard as he did. He had learned that great Renaissance painters such as Leonardo da Vinci served rigorous apprenticeships, so he expected the students to do the same. He assigned them to work alongside professional artists during the day and required them to study at night, seven days a week. After three years of this, they were to complete five years of intensive study, day and night. Few students or teachers had Rivera's energy and drive, so no one was happy with his plan, and Diego Rivera was soon fired.

He was also expelled from the Communist Party. Rivera had critics within the party who complained that he was too eager to paint murals for the government and too friendly with people in power. The party's leaders had taken an extreme position in response to government repression. As the party gained strength among peasants, government forces had beaten and killed union organizers. Some party members had been exiled to Islas Marías, an island prison colony. Rivera's expulsion was one of many as the party purged itself of anyone unwilling to toe the line. Kahlo, who had joined the party before marrying, appeared innocent of the charges against her husband. She was allowed to remain a member, but she chose to leave the party with him.

Rivera's critics nodded smugly when he accepted a commission from Dwight W. Morrow, the U.S. ambassador to Mexico. Morrow was a wealthy businessman who had worked out deals that let U.S. investors earn big profits in Mexico. He wanted to give something back to the Mexican people, though, so he hired Rivera to paint murals in the Palace of Cortés. This stone and concrete structure in the city of Cuernavaca looked like a European castle. It had been built in the 1500s by Indian stonecutters and carpenters forced to work by Hernán Cortés, the Spaniard who defeated the Aztec Empire and conquered large sections of Mexico. More than a hundred Indians had carried stone and timber down a mountain to the site.

Rivera boldly decorated the walls of the historic structure with scenes of conquest: Spaniards massacring native people and enslaved Indians suffering lashes from Spanish whips. One panel depicts Spanish friars forcing the Aztecs to convert to Christianity. Rivera showed the Indians who resisted conversion being hanged or burned to death. He painted sixteen scenes from Cuernavaca's history, ending with Emiliano Zapata leading peasants in revolt in the early twentieth century.

Ambassador Morrow had no problem with the panels showing Cortés and his army being cruel to the native people. But he worried about Rivera's paintings of Roman Catholic clergy putting Indians to death, even if everything the artist presented was true. Might these murals stir up trouble?

By 1927, Mexico's Catholics had spent three years protesting government action against their church without raising a hand or weapon. Some thought the time had come to arm themselves and fight back. Calling themselves Cristeros (fighters for Christ), they clashed violently with the Mexican army in Guanajuato and other towns. Cristeros captured by government forces were executed, but only after suffering gruesome torture. Their captors burned them with blow torches, broke the bones in their faces, and hung them up by their thumbs. The government shot or hanged Catholic priests, whether or not they played a role in the movement. Ninety thousand people died before the rebellion died down—Cristeros, soldiers, priests, and civilians.

Morrow had worked hard, using his skills as a diplomat to end the bloody conflict and bring about peace. The June 1929 agreement that he brokered allowed churches to open again. The last thing he wanted was for Rivera's wicked view of the church's early shameful role to cause new fighting. Please, Morrow asked, could Rivera paint just one priest doing good? Rivera complied and added Fray Toribio de Benevente, a monk who protected many Indians from Spanish abuse during the time of conquest.

A Rivera self-portrait from 1930.

Diego and Frida stayed in a luxurious home owned by Morrow and his wife in Cuernavaca, a city known for its mild climate and its gardens of flowers and fruit trees. Sometime in the early months of the marriage, Frida became pregnant. Her joy was brief, because her doctor found a problem with the way she was carrying the fetus, and she had an abortion. Thinking she might never be a mother, she cried hard and long. But she found comfort in her daily routine, in cooking, dusting, and being with Diego. And she began to paint again. She tended to make small paintings, portraits of Mexican Indian women and little girls. She made one painting of people seated on a bus. A housewife with her market basket, a laborer in overalls, a barefoot peasant woman nursing her baby, a well-dressed businessman—together, the passengers represent Mexican society.

Frida also turned dressing her body into an art. She gave up the fashions of 1930—the wavy hair, tailored suits, and straight skirts that fell to the mid-calf. She began to wear the traditional clothing of Tehuantepec, in southeast Mexico. The women of this region dressed colorfully in long, ruffled skirts and richly embroidered, boxy blouses called *huipiles*. They wrapped their braided hair around their heads and adorned it with ribbons and flowers. To these bright outfits Frida added rings, earrings, gold chains, bracelets, and heavy stone necklaces from the pre-Columbian era.

In November 1930, Diego and Frida boarded a train bound for California, because the city of San Francisco was hosting an exhibition of Rivera's paintings. Also, thanks to the efforts of sculptor Ralph Stackpole, Rivera had been hired to paint murals in the California School of Fine Arts (now the San Francisco Art Institute) and the luncheon club of the city's stock exchange. Investors made fortunes and lost them at the stock exchange. This kind of financial dealing—buying and selling shares in corporations—went against the collective principle of communism. But Rivera was eager for people in the United States to see his work, so he painted at the stock exchange anyway. He always did exactly as he pleased.

Frida called San Francisco "the City of the World" and felt thrilled to be making the trip. On the way north she gave Diego her newest self-portrait, painted against a city skyline. As they neared San Francisco and saw its buildings rising on the hills beyond, Diego had a big surprise. "I was almost frightened to realize that her imagined city was the very one we were now seeing for the first time," he explained. (The painting has since been lost.)

The couple stayed in Stackpole's roomy studio. Rivera hoped to capture the spirit of California in his murals, so he and Frida took in the sights of this charming city, which was like no other. They went to Fisherman's Wharf, where San Franciscans gathered to buy the day's catch. In the Mission District, they saw a Spanish-style church dedicated to the service of God in 1776; it reminded them that California, like Mexico, had once belonged to Spain. They saw sea lions on the rocky coast, and they went to a football game. Frida and Diego admired the spacious Victorian homes in the newer, western part of the city, but on other streets they saw men and women without money or hope. These Americans were struggling to make it through the Great Depression, which had begun the previous year, 1929.

This severe economic downturn would be brutal and long-lasting. Its impact on people's lives was already more drastic in the United States than it would ever be in Mexico. Rivera paused to sketch the hungry, out-of-work men who lined up on city sidewalks, waiting their turn for a free bowl of soup.

When Diego's work took him away from Frida, she explored San Francisco on her own. She toured museums and wandered through neighborhoods. She especially liked the section called Chinatown, because the immigrants who lived and worked there treated her kindly. "I've never seen more beautiful children in all my life than Chinese children," she wrote to Isabel Campos, a childhood friend from Coyoacán. Wherever she went, people stopped to stare at Frida in her Tehuana dress. Her splendid costumes let people know she was an original. For Frida they had another advantage: the long skirts hid her damaged leg.

Photographer Edward Weston, who had known Rivera in Mexico, saw the couple in San Francisco. He wrote in his diary about greeting the gargantuan artist again: "He took me clear off my feet in an embrace." Upon meeting Frida, Weston called her "a little doll alongside Diego, but a doll in size only, for she is strong and quite beautiful."

Out-of-work men pass the time on a San Francisco sidewalk. They are just a few
of the thousands of Americans who were unemployed during the Great Depression.

Frida found a lifelong friend when she consulted Dr. Leo Eloesser, the physician Diego had met in Mexico, about her right foot, which had been crushed in the accident and still caused pain. Like Frida, the forty-nine-year-old doctor was one of a kind. He spoke several languages, including Spanish. He played the viola and loved the arts so much that he treated musicians and artists free of charge. Small and dark-haired, he stood with his head thrust forward, always curious. He had unlimited energy and needed very little sleep, which may be why he liked nighttime sailing. Frida called him Doctorcito, or "dear little doctor."

Eloesser merely counseled Frida to rest and take good care of herself. Yet she felt grateful enough for his help to paint a portrait of Eloesser standing next to a model of his beloved sailboat. She valued his medical opinion as much as his friendship, and in the years ahead, as other doctors offered questionable treatments, she would often seek his advice.

To Eloesser, Frida was "a girl of unusual beauty. . . . Her hair was a lustrous black; her dark eyebrows almost met over her straight nose; her skin was of a light-coral pink." About Frida the artist he said, "Never did a painter, man or woman, so successfully transfer his (or her) emotions to canvas."

The artists spent six months in California while Rivera completed his murals. At the stock exchange he painted a giant woman, representing California.

Dr. Leo Eloesser treated Frida Kahlo when she visited San Francisco in 1930 and became her friend for life.

Within her great arms the woman cradled the fruit of California's farms, the state's miners and engineers, and the machinery that powered its factories. In his clever mural at the School of Fine Arts, titled *The Making of a Fresco*, Rivera painted himself sitting on a scaffold with his backside to the viewer, at work on a mural of people building a city. It was an example of trompe l'oeil, art designed to fool the eye, but San Franciscans hardly knew what to think of it. Was Rivera insulting them or just having fun? "If it is a joke, it is a rather amusing one, but in bad taste," commented Kenneth Callahan, a painter from Washington

State. Rivera's reason for choosing this subject was actually quite simple. It made sense to him that a mural painted in an art school should depict the way he made his art.

Frida was painting as well. She completed a picture titled *Frieda and Diego Rivera*, which is also known as *The Wedding Portrait*. In it, the artists stand side by side, holding hands. Diego is big and solid, whereas she is a tiny, delicate thing. That year, the San Francisco Society of Women Artists included *Frieda and Diego Rivera* in its annual show.

Once they returned to Mexico, Rivera used the money he earned in San Francisco to build a home for himself and Frida in a section of Mexico City called San Ángel. He built two houses, really—two modern cubes, a pink one for himself and a blue one for Frida. Rivera asked the architect who designed the houses, Juan O'Gorman, to make them spacious and useful, but at the lowest possible cost. O'Gorman did this by using functional elements in his design. This was why the electrical and plumbing systems were visible rather than hidden, as were the water tanks. It was why concrete-slab walls went unplastered. The houses, when built, "caused a sensation," O'Gorman said, "because a building whose form was completely derived from utilitarian construction had never been seen in Mexico." The home's design gave each artist private space for living and working, although Diego's house was bigger than Frida's. It featured a spacious studio with a wall of windows to let in abundant light. There was an ample kitchen, where the couple would eat most of their meals. If Diego wanted to go from his studio to Frida's rooftop terrace, he crossed a narrow bridge. Tall cactuses fenced the property to give the artists privacy.

Construction had barely started when Diego and Frida sailed back to the United States. This time they went to New York, where the Museum of Modern Art was hosting a show of Rivera's work. The museum's curators wanted patrons to see the murals that had made Rivera famous, but they could hardly tear walls out of buildings in Mexico and California and ship them to New York. So they came up with a different idea, and asked Rivera to complete a set of large frescoes right there in the city, and to paint them on panels that could be moved. They found him a studio, and he worked in his usual way, painting day and night. He re-created from memory scenes he had painted in Mexico. He also planned some new murals inspired by his impressions of New York.

While Diego worked, Frida spent long hours alone in the apartment that the museum

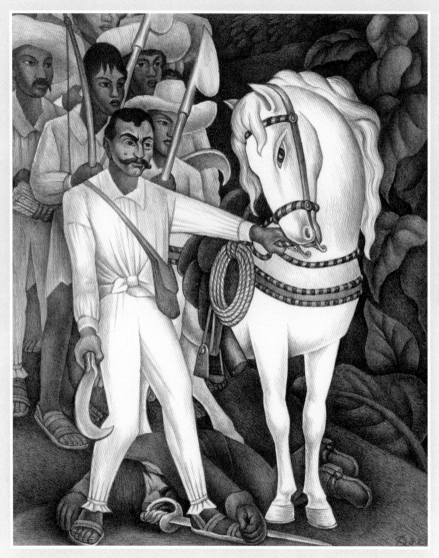

DIEGO RIVERA, *AGRARIAN LEADER ZAPATA*, 1931.

*In New York, Rivera painted the revolutionary Emiliano Zapata
as he had first painted him in Cuernavaca. Zapata stands on
the sword of a fallen oppressor beside his beautiful white horse.*

had provided. She saw Diego at the posh dinner parties the two were expected to attend. Diego mixed easily with high society and talked up a storm, but Frida felt out of place and suffered quietly through these long evenings. "I feel rage against all these rich people here, because I've seen thousands of people in the most terrible misery, without food and with no place to sleep," she wrote to Leo Eloesser. She complained that New Yorkers were cranky. New York, she said, was "an enormous, dirty chicken coop."

She felt even more distressed at one party as she watched the artist Lucienne Bloch, who was assisting Rivera while he created the frescoes, chatting merrily with Diego in French. Sunny Lucienne, who was two years younger than Frida, was a daughter of the acclaimed composer Ernest Bloch. As Frida watched the way Lucienne hung on Diego's every word, she grew furious. She made up her mind to silence this brazen flirt. Standing behind Bloch, she said in English, "I hate you." Lucienne Bloch turned and simply had to laugh. She assured Frida that she admired her husband's talent and personality but had no designs on him. She won Frida over, and the two women became good friends who toured the city and went to the movies together. Frida loved the popular comedies starring Laurel and Hardy or the Marx Brothers. And that new film *Frankenstein*, the one that was scaring so many people—Frida had to see it twice!

From New York the artists went to Detroit, Michigan, the next U.S. city that wanted murals by Diego Rivera. He had been hired to paint two panels in the garden court of the Detroit Institute of Arts. The Ford Motor Company was paying for the project, and Rivera could not have been happier. Detroit, the center of American automotive manufacturing, was just the place to depict "the great saga of the machine and of steel," he proclaimed. He gloried in the thirty-story Fisher Building, with golden tiles on its towering roof; the forty-seven-story Penobscot Building, the tallest skyscraper between New York and Chicago; and the mile-and-a-half-long Ambassador Bridge, which carried cars across the Detroit River to Canada.

As for Frida, "I don't like it *at all*," she wrote to Leo Eloesser. "The industrial part of Detroit is really the most interesting side, otherwise it's like the rest of the United States,

The Ford Motor Company's River Rouge complex was the largest factory in the world when it was completed, in 1928.

ugly and stupid." The main reason for Frida's letter, however, was to pass along some important news. "I am now *two* months pregnant," she told her doctor friend. She was also afraid. Concerned about carrying a baby in her damaged body, she had consulted a Detroit physician named Dr. Pratt. He told her she could enjoy a healthy pregnancy, but Frida had doubts. "What I want to know is your opinion, more than that of anyone else," she wrote. "I am willing to do what you think is best for my health, and *Diego agrees*." If Eloesser thought having a baby was too risky for her, then she would seek an abortion, despite the heartache that accompanied her first one. (The operation was illegal in the United States in 1932, but it was performed on many women nonetheless.)

Before Eloesser had a chance to reply, Frida made up her mind to have this baby. Dr. Pratt advised her to stay home and avoid activity, so Lucienne Bloch came from New York to keep Frida company. Diego hoped his wife would sit quietly and paint, but Frida felt restless in the hot, airless apartment where she and Diego were living. She had been learning to drive and was eager to practice; she wanted to go out and enjoy the few North American foods she liked: malted milk shakes, American cheese, and applesauce. Dr. Pratt, she told Lucienne, "tells me I can't do this, I can't do that, and that's a lot of bunk."

Rivera, meanwhile, toured drug and chemical companies. He spent a month at Ford's River Rouge plant, in nearby Dearborn, Michigan, sketching giant drill presses and conveyor belts. To him, this precision machinery was "as beautiful as the masterpieces of the ancient art of pre-columbian [sic] America." The ninety-three buildings at River Rouge had been designed to produce automobiles efficiently, without wasting money, time, or effort. Seventy-five thousand workers turned out four thousand Ford cars a day. As Rivera sketched, he thought about the undulating waves of electricity that drove the great machines, and how they rose and fell like the currents that moved through water, or the folded layers of rock that lay hidden in the earth. Wanting to paint this great continuity of ripples and curves, he envisioned a great series of murals. Instead of the two panels he had been hired to paint, he asked to cover twenty-seven.

He was nearly ready to start painting when something terrible happened. As June gave way to July, and Frida was in her fourth month of pregnancy, she lost the baby and began to bleed uncontrollably. Diego and Lucienne watched helplessly as she was rushed to a hospital. "She looked so tiny, twelve years old," Lucienne wrote in her diary. "Her tresses were wet with tears."

Frida spent thirteen days in Detroit's Henry Ford Hospital, her condition grave and her spirits low. In the years ahead she would have two more miscarriages, but neither would devastate her as this one did. Pencils and paints had helped her heal in the past, and now she longed to draw the child she had lost. She asked Dr. Pratt for a medical book with pictures of growing fetuses, but he denied her request, certain such pictures would upset her. When Diego learned of his refusal, he spoke up for Frida. "You are not dealing with an average person," he informed the doctor. "Frida will do something with it. She will do an artwork." He went out and bought a medical book for his wife, and she immediately sketched the unborn child whom she mourned.

Experiences, whether good or bad, cause people to gain self-knowledge. For artists, inner growth can lead to breakthroughs in their work, and this happened for Frida Kahlo. After leaving the hospital on July 17, she began to make paintings that were intensely symbolic and personal, revealing her innermost hopes, desires, and fears. In one of these paintings, *Henry Ford Hospital,* she lies naked on a bed in a pool of blood. Six cords emerge from her belly and are connected to various objects, among them a fetus, a pelvis, and a snail. Just as in a dream, the meaning is clearer for some of these objects than for others. The painting's setting adds to its dreamlike quality: Frida's bed rests on a flat, barren plain, under a blue sky, with Detroit's factories in the distance.

She also painted *Self-Portrait Between Mexico and the United States,* in which she presents herself in a ruffled pink dress, with the factories of Detroit on one side and the ancient ruins and flowers of Mexico on the other. Standing atop a stone block, she is at home in neither country. A Detroit journalist who interviewed her wrote, "She has acquired a very skillful and

Artist Lucienne Bloch, Rivera's assistant in New York, became Kahlo's close friend. She was photographed in Mexico when she traveled there with Kahlo in 1932.

beautiful style, painting in the small with miniature-like technique, which is so far removed from the heroic figures of Rivera as could well be imagined."

Rivera at last began to paint his sketches, even though he hated the architecture of the garden court of the Detroit Institute of Arts. It reminded him of Italian rooms from the seventeenth century, with wavy scrolls and figures from ancient myths carved into the molding. This ornate European style stood for "the way that we have clung to the old culture," he said. It went against the truly American art—representing Mexico and the United States, two American nations—that he was striving to produce. He wanted his murals to reflect "the stupendous creative effort of the workers from all races of the earth who make up the industrial population of Detroit and who symbolize the international, universal character of the American continent." Rivera had just one word for the raised stone fountain that burbled and splashed in the center of the garden court: *"horrorosa"* ("horrifying")!

On the twenty-seven panels, large and small, he painted iron and coal deposits deep underground. Giant hands reach up from the earth, grasping the metals needed to forge machinery. Workers build cars and airplanes, scientists develop life-saving drugs, and a doctor vaccinates a child with a serum the scientists have discovered. Rivera depicted the Great Lakes and inland waterways that carried the goods produced in Detroit to far-off markets. When many communists looked at Detroit's industry, they saw powerful capitalists getting rich from the labor of the working class. Rivera saw no conflict between his communist ideals and the factories and commerce he celebrated on these walls, however. In his mind, both communism and industry improved workers' lives.

September came, and Frida had just begun to feel well enough to join Diego in the garden court when a telegram from Mexico brought her dreadful news. Her mother was ill with cancer and near death. Frida tried to call her family in Coyoacán, but flooding on the Rio Grande had knocked out telephone communication between the United States and Mexico. Desperate to see her mother one last time, she made plans to go home. No flights connected Detroit and Mexico City, so she had to make the trip by train. Lucienne Bloch accompanied Frida, who was still too weak to travel alone.

For the first part of the journey, as the train clattered through Indiana, Illinois, and Missouri, Frida hid in a darkened compartment and cried. She wept for the child she lost, for the tiny, pretty mother she would soon lose, and for the husband she wished were near. The train reached the Mexican border only to be stopped by the flooding. After waiting twelve hours, the travel-weary passengers crossed into Mexico by bus. "The last hours were agony for her," Lucienne observed.

After seeing her mother on the morning of September 9, Frida could not be consoled. Although surrounded by her father and sisters, Frida "cries and cries and looks very pale," Lucienne noted in her diary. Frida communicated her sorrow and loneliness in letters to Diego in Detroit. She wrote in one letter, "Everything without you seems horrible to me. I am in love with you more than ever and at each moment more and more."

"I am very sad here without

In 1932, Kahlo and Rivera were happiest when they were together.

you," Diego replied. "Like you I can't even sleep and I hardly take my head away from work." He added, "Without you this life does not matter to me more than approximately two peanuts at most."

Matilde Calderón died a week after Frida reached Mexico, on September 15, 1932. Wrapped in dark shawls, all the sisters cried. Guillermo Kahlo, stunned, had trouble believing that his wife was really gone. During the five weeks they stayed on in Mexico, Frida and Lucienne took the grieving man for walks in a nearby park. They stayed with Frida's sister Matilde, and Frida brought Lucienne to San Ángel, to see the linked houses that were still being built. Frida explained the arrangement: "I can work, and he can work."

Diego Rivera lost a great deal of weight while Frida was in Mexico. He had changed so much that when Frida came back to Detroit, she failed to recognize the tall man with dark hair and protruding eyes who watched her step off the train. But as soon as she heard his voice, Frida knew who he was and ran into his arms.

With time Frida's health and happiness returned, and her old love of mischief surfaced. She sometimes behaved as though she were back in school, among the Cachuchas. At a stuffy tea with Detroit's high-society women, she sprinkled her conversation with curse words, pretending not to know what they meant. "What I did to those old biddies!" she later said to Diego, laughing as she told him about her day. At a formal dinner one night, Frida turned to Henry Ford, the founder of the Ford industrial empire and a known anti-Semite, to ask, "Mr. Ford, are you Jewish?" Diego almost choked on his food.

Diego was happier too with Frida at his side. Over the fall and winter, he finished his work at the Institute of Arts, and on March 13, 1933, people viewed the murals for the first time. Immediately this new work drew criticism. Some protesters called the frescoes "anti-American" and "Communistic," mostly out of a dislike for the artist's political beliefs and not because of the scenes he had depicted. Others had the opposite complaint. These people called the frescoes capitalistic and said they were a gigantic advertisement for the Ford Motor Company. At the same time, some religious leaders objected to the scene of the child being immunized, claiming it parodied European paintings of Christ's birth. The nurse and child in this panel appear to have halos, like the Virgin Mary and baby Jesus in religious works. Also, the horse, cow, and sheep that Diego placed in the foreground reminded them of the animals that, according to tradition, were present in the manger when Christ was born. Even before all this uproar, local artists had been demanding to know why Ford had hired a Mexican for the job rather than one of themselves. Cries rang out for the murals to be painted over.

Ridiculous, Rivera responded. Imagine Detroiters deploring "the pictorial representation of their city's existence and the source of its wealth, painted by a direct descendant of aboriginal American stock!" His inspiration was 100 percent American, he insisted. "If my Detroit frescoes are destroyed, I shall be profoundly distressed, as I put into them a year of my life and the best of my talent," he said, "but tomorrow I shall be busy making others, for I am not merely an 'artist,' but a man performing his biological function of producing paintings, just as a tree produces flowers and fruit."

6

WOUNDS

THE PRESIDENT of Ford Motor Company was Henry Ford's son, Edsel, a man who loved art as much as Rivera did. He spoke out publicly in support of the murals, saying, "I admire Rivera's spirit. I really believe he was trying to express his idea of the spirit of Detroit." Whether they agreed with Edsel Ford or the critics, thousands of people came to see the paintings. The frescoes' popularity protected them from being destroyed.

Rivera was already looking ahead to his next job, in New York City, for the powerful Rockefeller family. The Rockefellers began their rise in 1870, when John D. Rockefeller founded the Standard Oil Company with his brother William and several other partners. Rockefeller used bribes and deception to steal business away from competitors, so that by 1879, Standard Oil controlled 90 percent of U.S. oil refining. Rockefeller became one of the wealthiest people in the United States. In the decades that followed, the federal government passed laws regulating business practices in order to protect competition in the marketplace. No longer could Standard Oil or any other company control an industry. Nevertheless, John D. Rockefeller remained a very rich man. He and his family used some of their fortune to finance large construction projects such as Colonial Williamsburg in Virginia and the Museum of Modern Art in New York.

The Rockefellers had hired Rivera to paint a mural in the RCA Building, a thick slab of stone and glass scraping the city sky. Today it is called the GE Building, but in 1933, when it was new, this seventy-story office tower was named for its main tenant, the Radio Corporation of America. It was part of Rockefeller Center, a business and entertainment complex in Midtown Manhattan that remains popular with tourists. The Rockefellers financed the construction of Rockefeller Center between 1930 and 1939. Its fourteen original buildings included Radio City Music Hall, where audiences enjoyed movies and live shows. City residents and tourists still gather in the center's sunken plaza, where a gilded statue of the Greek god Prometheus gleams in the sun.

New Yorkers were so curious about Rivera that the Rockefellers sold tickets to people wanting to watch him work. He was painting a tremendous mural, sixty-three feet long and seventeen feet high, with a mighty theme:

The RCA Building adds its light to the nighttime glow of Midtown Manhattan in 1933.

Man at the Crossroads Looking with Hope and High Vision to the Choosing of a New and Better Future. Having begun painting in late March, Rivera applied pigments furiously, hoping to complete the mural by May. On its left side he painted everything he thought was wrong in the United States of America in 1933. Corporate fat cats danced and played cards, while police brutalized poor people and striking workers. To the right, ordinary Americans from different walks of life—laborers, farmers, teachers, parents, and children—worked together to build the new and better world. Glorious science, at the mural's center, was the great engine that drove progress. Its microscopes opened up the unseen world of disease-causing microbes, and its telescopes revealed the secrets of planets and stars.

The work progressed smoothly for a month, until April 24, when the *New York World-Telegram* announced, "Rivera Paints Scenes of Communist Activity." The newspaper revealed that red, the color of communism, dominated in one section of Rivera's mural: "waves of red headdress and of red flags in a victorious on-sweep." This was shocking news in the United States of the Great Depression, when many people believed communism threatened their peaceful, democratic way of life. Communists were leading strikes that sometimes resulted in bloodshed. Communists were also holding demonstrations, including a hunger march that brought sixteen hundred people to the steps of the U.S. Capitol. There was real concern that communism, which promised every citizen a share in the nation's wealth, might attract young people who were reaching adulthood and finding the doors of opportunity locked and barred. Who knew what would happen if angry youth took to the streets? Would there be violence? Would protesters demand that the state take ownership of the nation's factories, as the Soviet government had done?

Worried about protests and possible violence, the Rockefellers stopped selling tickets and posted guards in the RCA Building, but they assured Rivera that he could keep on painting as he wished. They reasoned that if his murals in San Francisco and Detroit had gained the public's approval, then this one would too, once the furor died down. Besides, in the long run a little controversy was bound to draw tourists to Rockefeller Center. No longer performing for a paying audience, Rivera hung big sheets of paper to block himself and his mural from prying eyes.

Then he went too far. In his zeal for communism, and believing he had the Rockefellers' solid support, he gave a union boss in his mural the face of Vladimir Lenin, the first leader of the Soviet Union.

On May 4 he received a letter from John D. Rockefeller's twenty-four-year-old grandson, Nelson, who had dropped by the RCA Building and peeked at the mural. Nelson Rockefeller praised the beauty of Rivera's painting, but the Lenin portrait might very easily "seriously offend a great

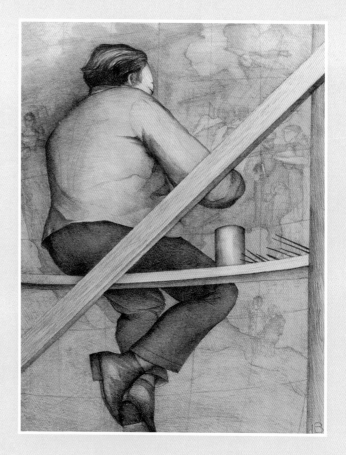

Lucienne Bloch sketched Rivera as he balanced on a scaffold and worked on his mural.

many people," he wrote. "As much as I dislike to do so, I am afraid we must ask you to substitute the face of some unknown man where Lenin's face now appears." Red flags and head scarves could be open to interpretation, but there was no mistaking the meaning of Lenin's presence.

What? Were the Rockefellers really asking him to change what he had painted? Rivera's mural was nearly complete, and Lenin's portrait was just one small part of it. Painting over the face would be easy, and it would please his employers. But Rivera chose this moment to stand up for his ideals. Suppose he agreed to this change and then the Rockefellers asked for more—did he risk losing creative control? Rivera made up his mind, and on May 6 he sent a letter of reply to Nelson Rockefeller. Lenin would stay where he was, Rivera wrote. He offered to make other concessions, perhaps replacing the dancing rich people with "a figure of some great American historical leader, such as Abraham Lincoln." But rather than make the specific change Rockefeller had asked for, he claimed that he "should prefer the physical destruction of the conception in its entirety."

There is an old saying: Be careful what you wish for. On May 9 the Rockefellers paid Diego Rivera in full for his mural and promptly fired him. In a move that infuriated lovers of artistic freedom, they had carpenters hammer tarpaper and wooden screening over the mural. Three hundred angry protesters picketed Rockefeller Center, calling out, "Freedom in art!" and "Save Rivera's painting!" Some enraged marchers demanded to see Nelson Rockefeller with a rope around his neck. As people marched in Midtown Manhattan, mounted police officers beat them back with clubs. Meanwhile, a group of artists and writers took a quieter approach and sent a petition to Rockefeller, asking him to rethink his position.

There was no chance. The Rockefellers wanted nothing more to do with Rivera or his mural. They promised, however, that "the uncompleted fresco of Diego Rivera will not be destroyed, nor in any way mutilated." It would merely "be covered to remain hidden for an indefinite time." The uproar in New York raised a current of doubt that moved across the land like winds rustling midwestern corn. It reached the directors of the General Motors Corporation, who had arranged for Rivera to paint a mural at the 1933 Chicago World's Fair. Fearing controversy, these stately gentlemen promptly canceled his contract.

Rivera went on the radio to plead his case to the American people. A work of art was "the property of all humanity," he said, and "no individual owner has the right to destroy it or keep it solely for his own enjoyment." He vowed to use his profit from the Rockefeller project, which amounted to seven thousand dollars, to paint another mural in New York City. After inspecting several sites, he painted a series of scenes from U.S. history at the New Workers' School, a communist institution. In this work, Rivera presented a unique view of American history, one that culminated in another portrait of Vladimir Lenin. It also included sinister portrayals of Adolf Hitler and Benito Mussolini. As the leaders of Nazi

Bloch also managed to photograph Man at the Crossroads, *Rivera's controversial unfinished mural, before the Rockefellers covered it. This picture shows the gears, wheels, and levers at the mural's center. The bearded Lenin is to the right, beneath the swirling galaxies.*

Germany and Fascist Italy, these two men preached an extreme form of nationalism that targeted people with ethnic backgrounds or beliefs different from their own. Within a few years their hatred of minorities and greed for power would cost millions of people their lives and lead to another world war.

Because the school was old and soon to be torn down, Rivera created his murals on movable panels. They were "the best that I have painted," he boasted, but the head of the school, Bertram Wolfe, thought otherwise. Wolfe later observed that the artist made the same claim about every mural he painted. These frescoes, Wolfe said, were far from his best.

Soon after breaking ties with the Rockefellers, Diego and Frida moved out of the hotel suite where they had been staying and into a two-room apartment near the New Workers' School. Friends flowed in and out of the small flat in a free and easy way. At the home of Diego Rivera and Frida Kahlo, the wealthy mixed as equals with ordinary laborers. "All were treated like one body of people. It was very simple," recalled an artist named Louise Nevelson, who was one of Rivera's assistants. Many nights Rivera treated the group to dinner at an Italian or Chinese restaurant.

It was a happy time for all until Rivera singled out the beautiful Nevelson for special attention. "I, unfortunately, was not a faithful husband," he admitted. "I was always encountering women too desirable to resist." Many women were drawn to Rivera, although he was hardly a handsome man; in fact, more than one person compared his face to a frog's. But Louise Nevelson said, "If a man's a genius, I don't care what he looks like," and it may be that other women felt the same way. Once the affair began, Rivera would stay out at night until sunrise, and the crowd stopped coming.

Lucienne Bloch saw what was happening and was furious for her friend's sake. Frida was "too perfect a person for anyone to have the strength to take her place," Bloch believed. If Lucienne knew about the affair, then Frida had to know as well. She chose to stay with Diego despite his infidelity, but people today can only guess at her reasoning. She may have hoped he would change one day and be faithful to her. Or she may have wanted to be with Diego so much that she was willing to suffer the pain he caused her.

Frida's foot hurt, so she seldom went out. She spent hours in the bathtub, seeking relief from the summer heat and thinking about her life. She reached one conclusion: it was time to go home to Mexico.

Diego disagreed. He liked living in the United States, and not simply because Nevelson was there. He was making friends with influential people who could help his career. The United States was bigger and more powerful than Mexico, so by painting in U.S. cities, he exposed more people to his work and his political message. This was important, he maintained, because when the world's workers rose up in revolt, it was bound to happen in a wealthy industrialized country like the United States. "The buildings which today have been erected out of the capitalist drive for profits" — the buildings where he painted his murals — "will tomorrow, because of their public functional utility, be delivered over into the hands of the workers." He advised Frida to bear with her homesickness for the good of communism.

Bunk! yelled Frida. All through the fall, she and Diego argued about whether to stay or to go. The loudest shouting matches left Frida trembling, but at least she could use art to express how out of place she felt. She cut out pictures of tall buildings and the Statue of Liberty to make a collage of New York City. She included a gasoline pump and a smokestack to represent U.S. industry, and she added a trash can overflowing with the debris of human suffering to stand for the people crushed by the Depression. In the collage, one pillar holds up a toilet and

Louise Nevelson, shown here around 1931, became a world-renowned sculptor. She is best known for her large cupboard-like wooden constructions.

another supports a sports trophy, as if these are highly prized objects. A Tehuana dress hangs on a clothesline between them. The picture's title, *My Dress Hangs There,* is a clue to its meaning. The dress may be in New York, but where is the woman who wore it? In her mind she is far away.

New York grew cold. Finally it was December, and the panels at the New Workers' School were complete. Rivera's romance with Nevelson had run its course, and Nevelson was eager to move forward with her life and artistic career. "I had my future in front of me, and I was very confident that I could fulfill it," she said. Rivera painted two more pictures for the Manhattan headquarters of a communist organization. Only then, after he had spent all the money he had received from the Rockefellers, did he agree to go home. He and Frida sailed for Mexico on December 20, 1933.

Within months, the Rockefellers had Rivera's mural taken down, breaking their promise to the artist and the world. Because Rivera had created a true fresco, mixing pigments with wet plaster, the only way to remove it was to chip it away, one small piece at a time.

Rivera, however, got an artist's revenge. He repainted the lost mural in the Palace of Fine Arts in Mexico City. Not only did he include Vladimir Lenin this time, but he also painted John D. Rockefeller, Jr., Nelson's father, among the capitalists partying on the mural's left side. Close to Rockefeller he placed swimming spirochetes, the bacteria that cause syphilis, to imply that the family was tainted. Their wealth was like a disease. (Nelson Rockefeller went on to become governor of New York from 1959 through 1973, and vice president of the United States from 1974 until 1977. He also became a noted art collector.)

In Mexico, Frida and Diego made peace with each other, and for a little while they lived tranquilly in the two houses in San Ángel. Most days they ate a late breakfast together before Diego went to his studio to paint. Frida either painted or visited one of her friends or sisters until lunchtime, when the home in San Ángel became a festive gathering place. Artists, writers, and performers — people such as U.S. novelist John Dos Passos and Mexican film star Dolores del Rio — sat around a colorful table that Frida had arranged with flowers, fruit, and pottery. In the Kahlo-Rivera household, anything could happen. When California artist Marjorie Eaton came to lunch in 1934, a spider monkey sat on her head and snatched a banana right out of her hand. "I had to balance the monkey, whose tail was around my neck, as I was showing my sketches," Eaton said. Frida loved animals, and for the rest of her life would keep a noisy, mischievous collection of pets that included monkeys, parrots, the Mexican hairless dogs known as *itzcuintli,* and a small deer.

During this otherwise carefree time Frida was in and out of the hospital. She had surgery on her foot, she had her appendix removed, and she had another abortion for medical reasons. Knowing she might never have a baby of her own, she doted on her sister Cristina's daughter and son, Isolda and Antonio. Cristina's husband had left her, and she was living with Guillermo Kahlo in the blue house in Coyoacán. Frida bought presents for the children, and she paid for their schooling and music and dancing lessons.

As Frida struggled to be cheerful, Diego let her know that he was depressed. He missed the United States, where he had been a celebrity, and he blamed Frida for his unhappiness. He halfheartedly went back to the National Palace to complete his stairway murals, and he invited Cristina and her children to pose for him. Then, as in the past, he began an affair with his model. But this time the model was Frida's sister.

Frida had managed to forgive Diego for being involved with Louise Nevelson. His cheating hurt, but Nevelson meant nothing to her. Yet for her husband and her sister, the two people closest and dearest to her, to carry on a secret romance—this betrayal was almost too much to bear. "It costs me very dearly to go through this," Frida confided in Leo Eloesser. "You can't have any idea of what I suffer. Everything that is happening to me is so complicated that I don't know how to explain it to you."

Her sadness, frustration, and rage were too strong to hold inside. She grabbed a big pair of scissors and chopped off her long hair. She bundled up her Tehuana skirts and stuffed them away in a closet—she was in no mood to wear them. Needing to paint, she found the perfect subject in a newspaper story about a murdered woman. The victim's

Modern-day visitors stand on the high walkway that links the separate houses of Diego Rivera and Frida Kahlo in San Ángel.

boyfriend, in a drunken rage, had taken a knife and riddled her body with stab wounds. Hauled before a judge, the man played down what he had done, insisting, "It was just a few little pricks!" Kahlo made a small painting of the crime scene and titled it *A Few Small Nips.* To depict the killing in all its goriness, she painted splatters of blood on the picture's wooden frame.

Frida's wounds were emotional, but they cut her just as deeply. In early 1935, after Diego paid for Cristina to have a home of her own, Frida finally left him. Taking a pet spider monkey along for company, she moved from San Ángel to an apartment in Mexico

City. She spent the next summer in New York, seeing Lucienne Bloch and other friends. Observing her life from this great distance, Frida understood that she still loved Diego and he loved her. The affair with Cristina would end, and he would have others; he was never going to change. "I cannot love him for what he is not," she concluded. So she forgave both Diego and Cristina, although the affair had not yet waned, and when fall came, she went back to San Ángel. She returned stronger, more independent, and vowing to live a meaningful life on her own terms. She put on her Tehuana skirts, and she let her hair grow long again.

In one of the rare moments when he spoke honestly about his character flaws, Rivera said, "If I loved a woman, the more I loved her, the more I wanted to hurt her. Frida was only the most obvious victim of this disgusting trait."

A turbulent love kept husband and wife together, but so did art, and so did politics. For nearly ten years, Diego and Frida had been following the news about Leon Trotsky. Once a leading figure in the Soviet Communist Party, Trotsky had become a man without a country. In 1927, after criticizing Joseph Stalin, the party's general secretary and the most powerful man in the Soviet Union, Trotsky was expelled from the party. Stalin was a cruel and ironfisted leader who tolerated no dissent. Anyone who spoke out against Stalin or his policies would be sent to a *gulag* (forced-labor camp), where starvation and brutality were the way of life, or exiled to Siberia, or killed. Terrified of enemies real or imagined, Stalin had millions of Soviet citizens put to death. In 1929 Trotsky was forced to flee. In his absence the Soviet government staged a series of trials that were rigged to frame him for plotting from abroad to assassinate Stalin. As a result, Trotsky lived under a death sentence. Anytime, anywhere, Stalin's supporters might track him down and execute him.

Since his exile, Trotsky had lived in Turkey, France, and Norway, yet he was never welcomed in those countries or allowed to settle permanently. In 1936, Rivera had a letter from Anita Brenner, a Mexican-born writer living in the United States, asking if Mexico might take

Trotsky in. Trotsky and his wife of thirty-five years, Natalia, were desperate, Brenner wrote. Country after country had denied them entry, and they had nowhere to turn.

Many communists overlooked Stalin's ruthlessness because they were eager for the Soviet Union to succeed, but Diego Rivera was not among them. He deplored the cold-blooded way Stalin had dissenters killed or locked away in prisons and labor camps. Echoing Trotsky, Rivera called Stalin "the Undertaker of the Revolution." He also hated Stalin's suppression of the arts. Any painting displayed or book published in the Soviet Union had to glorify the nation and its leaders. Artists who painted outside the approved lines risked their lives. Rivera also believed Trotsky had a right to live in freedom and safety. So even though Rivera was ill at the time with eye and kidney ailments, he called on Mexico's president, Lázaro Cárdenas, and asked him to grant Trotsky asylum. To his surprise, Cárdenas agreed to his request. The president believed that inviting Trotsky to Mexico was the decent thing to do.

This was how the Trotskys came to step ashore in Mexico on January 9, 1937. They traveled secretly by train to Mexico City, because Leon Trotsky was constantly in danger, even in Mexico. The Mexican Communist Party, which supported Stalin, had hung posters throughout the city demanding, OUT WITH TROTSKY, THE ASSASSIN. Of course, Rivera's support for Trotsky gave party members another reason to criticize him.

The Trotskys were to stay in Coyoacán; Guillermo Kahlo went to live with his daughter Adriana and let them move into the blue house. Rivera bought the empty lot next door and hired guards to patrol the property day and night, to make it harder for snipers to get near. Yet in Coyoacán it was easy to believe that danger was far away. The Trotskys ventured out to tour Mexico City and to socialize with Diego and Frida and other friends. They felt settled for the first time in years, and they loved their surroundings. "We were on a new planet in Rivera's house," Natalia said.

In Diego Rivera, Leon Trotsky saw a true communist revolutionary artist at work. "Do you wish to see with your own eyes the hidden springs of the social revolution?" he asked.

"Look at the frescoes of Rivera. Do you wish to know what revolutionary art is like? Look at the frescoes of Rivera." Trotsky also admired Rivera's wife. In fact, he was smitten with Frida. He wrote love notes in English and hid them in books that he passed along to her to read. Frida felt drawn to this worldly, handsome man with keen blue eyes. She called him Piochitas (Little Goatee) because she liked his small white beard. Kahlo was twenty-nine and Trotsky was fifty-eight when they began meeting secretly at the home of Cristina, in whom Frida had confided.

But why did Frida have this affair? It might seem that she wanted to get even with Diego, to hurt him as much as he had hurt her. To be betrayed by his wife and the famous man he had done so much to help was bound to cause him anguish and shame. Yet Frida

Kahlo and Max Schachtman, leader of the American Communist Committee (right), welcome Natalia and Leon Trotsky to Mexico.

concealed the romance from him, fearing his jealousy. She knew that her husband lived by a double standard when it came to extramarital affairs. It was fine for him to carry on with any woman who caught his eye, but his wife was not to be involved with other men. Frida worried that an angry Diego might throw the Trotskys out of the blue house. He still owned his pistol—might he be driven to assassinate Leon Trotsky himself? It was much better not to find out. A more likely reason for the affair was Frida's newfound independence. She simply felt attracted to Trotsky and wanted to be with him.

Trotsky's wife understood what was happening, though, and the knowledge pierced her heart. Natalia had "one of the saddest faces I have ever seen," remarked James T. Farrell, a writer from Chicago who saw her at this time. Farrell, a Trotsky supporter, had come to Mexico to observe the proceedings of an international commission that was looking into the Moscow trials. The commission held its hearings in the blue house, beginning in April 1937. Farrell and the rest of the world watched as Trotsky responded to the charges against him and presented evidence to prove them false. He had "an extremely fertile and quick mind," Farrell said, "throwing off ideas right and left, constantly and continually, shifting from subject to subject, analyzing the most minute details." Trotsky ended his testimony by declaring that Stalin's Political Bureau was "composed of falsifiers." He cleared his name and won supporters in many countries, but his words angered Joseph Stalin, who vowed anew to have him eliminated. One way or another, Stalin would succeed.

By July, the love affair between Leon Trotsky and Frida Kahlo had grown cold. Trotsky hated making his wife suffer, and Kahlo admitted to a friend in New York, "I am really tired of the old man." Still, she remained fond of him, and on his birthday, November 7, she gave him a painting. It was a portrait of herself elegantly dressed in a peach and red Tehuana costume, holding a bouquet and standing between two heavy white curtains.

Trotsky left the painting behind when he and Natalia abruptly left the blue house in April 1939. The friendship between Leon Trotsky and Diego Rivera had ended suddenly—and badly. Publicly, Rivera blamed political differences, but the true reason for the breach was personal. Somehow Rivera had learned of Trotsky's affair with Kahlo. Instead of losing his temper, as Frida had feared, he reacted with calculated anger. He ordered Trotsky out and warned that if the great man failed to cooperate, he was prepared to tell the world that Trotsky had betrayed not only Natalia but also those who had reached out to help him. The old Soviet freedom fighter had no choice but to move with his wife into another fortified suburban home.

7

LIFE'S BITTERNESS

❀

THE YEARS 1937 and 1938 had been a time of growth for Kahlo the artist. She had painted steadily and produced some of her best-known works. Among them was *Remembrance of an Open Wound,* in which Kahlo presented herself with her skirt raised to display her bandaged, bleeding foot. The painful ulcer that made her need the bandage was all too real. But in the painting Kahlo also showed herself with a gaping cut on her thigh, an injury she never actually suffered. It is likely that this open wound symbolized emotional distress. The painting *My Nurse and I* — one of Kahlo's favorites — reflects her interest in Mexicanidad. The nurse in this painting is an Indian woman wearing a dark pre-Columbian mask. Here Kahlo painted herself with an adult's head and a child's body, taking nourishment from the nurse's breast. In this symbolic way, Kahlo showed Mexico feeding her creativity.

Another intriguing painting from 1938 is *What the Water Gave Me.* In this work Kahlo took the thoughts and memories that passed through her mind as she bathed and turned them into images floating in the tub. Her father and mother obscured by leafy growth, a Tehuana dress, a sailboat like Leo Eloesser's, a skyscraper emerging from a volcano — these and other pictures drift in the water over the bather's legs. As in *Henry Ford Hospital* (the painting Kahlo completed in Detroit after her miscarriage), some of these images are easier to interpret than others.

To see his wife produce such original work delighted Diego Rivera, and he did all he could to further her career. When the noted Hollywood actor and art collector Edward G. Robinson came to San Ángel, Rivera persuaded him to buy four of Kahlo's paintings, at about two hundred dollars apiece. To Rivera, the contradictions in Kahlo's work were what made it so intriguing. Her paintings were "acid and tender, hard as steel and delicate and fine as a butterfly's wing," he wrote, "loveable [sic] as a beautiful smile, and profound and cruel as the bitterness of life."

Kahlo liked the attention. People were starting to view her as an important artist in her own right, not just as the great muralist's little wife, a mere dabbler in art. She also liked the cash she was earning and what it could do for her. "I can be free to travel and do whatever I want without asking Diego for money," she said.

With Rivera's encouragement, Kahlo submitted some paintings to a group show that was held in early 1938 in Mexico City. There they caught the eye of Julien Levy, a leading New York art dealer. Levy was so excited by what he saw that he immediately began planning an exhibition of Kahlo's work for his Manhattan gallery. The paintings also electrified the French writer André Breton, who had come to Mexico with his wife, the artist Jacqueline Lamba. Breton loved Kahlo's strange, original images, painted so delicately. "The art of Frida Kahlo is a ribbon wrapped around a bomb," he proclaimed.

Breton was a founder of the artistic movement known as Surrealism, which arose in Europe after World War I. Inspired by Sigmund Freud's exploration of the unconscious, the Surrealists wanted to see what would emerge from their brushes and pens if they let ideas pour dreamlike from their minds. In the Surrealist paintings of Salvador Dalí, René Magritte, and other artists, melting clocks hang from dead branches, or a green apple might float in the air, hiding the face of a man in a bowler hat. Surrealists strived, Breton said, "to present interior reality and exterior reality as two elements in the process of unification, of finally becoming one."

To Breton, Kahlo was a natural Surrealist, but the artist herself was uneasy with the

Russian-American artist Misha Reznikoff painted The Solidity of the Road to Metaphor and Memory *in 1935. Like other Surrealist works, this painting depicts a scene and figures that seem to have come from a dream. Frida Kahlo insisted that she was not a Surrealist because she painted real people and images that sprang from her conscious, waking mind.*

label. "I never knew I was a Surrealist till André Breton came to Mexico and told me I was," she said. "The only thing I know is that I paint because I need to, and I paint always whatever passes through my head, without any other consideration." Breton also wanted to show her paintings in his country, but the New York exhibition at Julien Levy's gallery came first.

Levy promised that his show would feature paintings combining "a native Mexican quality which is naïve, an unusual female frankness and intimacy, and a sophistication which is the surrealist element." He added, "The work of this newcomer is decidedly important and threatens even the laurels of her distinguished husband." Leading people from the New York art world crowded Levy's gallery on November 1, opening night. Artists, critics, and collectors were curious to see these paintings and meet the woman in folkloric dress who had created them.

Frida's costume still caused a stir wherever she went. One day in New York, Julien Levy saw several children follow her into a bank, wanting to know where the circus was. She was a "mythical creature, not of this world," Levy said, "proud and absolutely sure of herself, yet terribly soft." He noticed that Kahlo's health limited her activity. She would rather sit in a café and watch passersby than stroll along sidewalks or tour a museum, because walking pained her. By the end of the day she was too tired to enjoy the city's nightlife.

Her art drew attention and gained her fans. About half the paintings in Julien Levy's gallery sold. The art impressed the well-known writer Clare Boothe Luce, who commissioned Kahlo to paint a portrait of her late friend Dorothy Hale. The young, beautiful Hale had fallen into the deepest despair after her husband died and left her in debt, and her dreams of an acting career had been dashed. She told her friends that she was leaving on a long trip, and on October 20, 1938, she hosted a farewell cocktail party. Early the next morning, she jumped to her death from the sixteenth floor of the Hampshire House apartment building, where she lived.

Luce wanted to give the painting to Hale's mother as a remembrance. She expected Kahlo to paint something elegant and pretty, like the portrait she did of herself for Leon Trotsky. So when Luce received the painting and removed it from its crate, she was shocked and physically ill. Kahlo had painted the suicide in gruesome detail and in stages, as if it had happened in slow motion. She showed Hale first leaving the window, looking small and far away; then tumbling through the clouds and drawing nearer; and finally lying on the pavement in a black velvet dress, bloody and dead. The blood drips onto the frame, as in *A Few Small Nips*. Although Luce could never give *The Suicide of Dorothy Hale* to the dead woman's mother, she understood that Kahlo had created a highly original work of art. After keeping it in its crate for several years, she donated the painting anonymously to the Phoenix Art Museum.

In New York, away from Diego Rivera, Frida experimented with life as an independent artist. She was often with Nickolas Muray, a successful portrait photographer. Born in Hungary, Muray was a suave, athletic man who had won a bronze medal in fencing at the 1932 Olympics. Kahlo and Muray grew close as he helped her get ready for the gallery show. Together they unpacked her paintings, which had been shipped to New York from Mexico. Muray advised Kahlo on how they should be hung, and he photographed them for her. He viewed photography as more than a profession. It was "a contact between people," he said, and he used it "to understand human nature and record, if possible, the best in each individual." His portraits of Kahlo are among his most famous images.

Even as Frida began a romance with Nickolas Muray, there were moments when she missed Diego and felt the full strength of her love for him. She turned to him in January 1939, when it was time to sail for France for her exhibition there and she felt afraid to go so far away because of her health. Diego gave her the assurance she needed. He wrote from Mexico in capital letters, "TAKE FROM LIFE ALL WHICH SHE GIVES YOU, WHATEVER IT MAY BE, PROVIDED IT IS INTERESTING AND CAN GIVE YOU SOME PLEASURE." He also reminded her, "When one is old, one knows what it is to have lost what offered itself when one did not know enough to take it."

Paris, when Frida arrived, was a city on edge. Adolf Hitler's Nazi forces had moved beyond Germany's borders to invade Austria and a section of Eastern Europe known as the Sudetenland. As Parisians watched and waited for Hitler to turn his attention to France, life went uneasily on. Artists still set up their easels beside the river Seine. The cathedral of Notre Dame de Paris, with its stone towers and arching buttresses, was as breathtaking as ever. People walking along the city's streets savored the mingled aromas of coffee, garlic, fresh-baked bread, and flowers.

At first Frida stayed with Jacqueline Lamba and André Breton in their small apartment, sharing their little girl's bedroom. She expected the show to open shortly, but problems kept cropping up. First, the French customs office held her paintings for several weeks. Then Breton decided to make the paintings part of a bigger exhibition of Mexican art, one that included pre-Columbian pieces, nineteenth-century works, and pictures by Mexican photographer Manuel Bravo. The old paintings needed to be restored, but this took time—and money, with Breton having to borrow two hundred dollars from his guest. Frida was running out of patience. The people she met either failed to make good on their promises or put on airs, trying to sound learned. "I decided to send everything to hell, and scram from this rotten Paris before I get nuts myself," she wrote to Nickolas Muray.

Refined, worldly Nickolas Muray became Kahlo's lover when she was living in New York.

She remained, however, in part because she was too ill to travel. A kidney infection sent her to a hospital. When she was released, she went to stay with a woman from the United States named Mary Reynolds, who was living with the artist Marcel Duchamp. She wrote to friends that she liked Duchamp better than the "s. of a b.," as she called Breton. She also found things to like about France, from the wondrous Gothic cathedral at Chartres, famed for its magnificent stained-glass windows, to the Paris flea markets, where she bought a pair of antique dolls.

When the art exhibition, which Breton titled *Mexique*, finally opened in March, Kahlo scored a big hit with her seventeen paintings and her colorful self. She was honored when the Louvre purchased one of her self-portraits for its collection, a painting of Kahlo with yellow blossoms in her hair and framed by flowers and birds. It now hangs in the same museum that houses the *Mona Lisa*, the ancient Greek statue known as *Winged Victory*, and other world-famous art treasures.

Diego's old friend Pablo Picasso was so taken with Frida that he gave her tortoise-shell earrings carved in the shape of hands. He taught her a Spanish song, "El Huérfano" ("The Orphan"), which became a favorite of hers, one she would sing for Diego and friends in Mexico.

Finally her paintings had been shown, and Frida could leave Paris. On March 25, she

Pablo Picasso was photographed in his Paris studio in 1939. The original caption for this picture stated that the artist "was dressed more neatly than usual."

sailed for New York, the first stop on her journey home. There Nickolas Muray stunned her with the news that their romance was over. He had met another woman, one he would marry. Muray had always known, he said, that he came second to Rivera in Frida's affections. "Of the three of us there were only two of you," he told her. Frida spent a month in New York, healing her broken heart, before going home to San Ángel.

Roughly four months later, on September 1, 1939, Germany invaded Poland. France and Great Britain responded by declaring war on Germany. This declaration marked the start of World War II in Europe. On June 14, 1940, Parisians saw the sight they had been dreading: Hitler's forces entering their city.

That fall Frida was living on her own in Coyoacán. *Time* magazine reported that the "toad-shaped Mexican muralist otherwise known as Diego Rivera" and Frida Kahlo, the "svelte German-Mexican modernist painter, classed by Diego as among the four or five best in the world," were seeking a divorce. They kept the reason for the split private and appeared calm and even cheerful when questioned by reporters. Speaking with a monkey perched on his shoulder, Rivera insisted there was no problem. "There is no change in the magnificent relations between us," he boasted. They were divorcing, he said, for "legal convenience in the spirit of modern times"—whatever that might mean. Kahlo said only, "We were not getting along well." Yet the press had been full of gossip about Rivera and the Hollywood film star Paulette Goddard. Diego pursued one woman after another, and Frida knew it.

Whether he learned of Frida's romance with Muray is unknown, but he had found out about her involvement with Trotsky, and she was said to have had other brief affairs, some with men and others with women. In this marriage there may have been too much betrayal, and too much pain, for either partner to forgive or forget. The divorce became final on November 6, 1939. Rivera was nearly fifty-three, and Kahlo was thirty-two.

As if pretending that everything was fine could make it so, Diego and Frida put on a show of being on good terms. They entertained friends together and went with them to the theater. Arrayed in brilliant clothes and jewelry, Frida glittered and laughed in the

DIEGO RIVERA, *PORTRAIT OF PAULETTE GODDARD*, 1940–41.

Rivera painted this portrait of Paulette Goddard attended by a Mexican woman.

public eye, but later her only audience was her heart, which ached for Diego's love, and her only companion was a bottle of cognac. She painted a dual self-portrait, in which two Fridas sit side by side, holding hands. One wears an old-fashioned white bridal dress; the other is in Tehuana garb. Their hearts are exposed and connected by a blood vessel, to signify that they are one, yet both Fridas suffer. The Frida in white has severed a vein, which bleeds onto her dress. The Tehuana Frida holds a miniature portrait of Diego as a child, a symbol of her loss. Again Kahlo cut her hair, and she painted herself in a man's suit, in a flat, barren place, with her black locks littering the ground. She worked harder than ever at her art, wanting to earn enough money to support herself.

How Frida could care so deeply for a man who caused her such anguish is hard to

FRIDA KAHLO, *THE TWO FRIDAS*, 1939.

A woman studies The Two Fridas, *which was exhibited at the Los Angeles County Museum of Art in 2012.*

understand. Her love for Diego had become an obsession. He was on her mind day and night. She craved affection from him even as she tried to build a new life for herself.

Rivera adjusted more easily to life after the divorce, or so it appeared. He spent as much time as he could in his studio, painting. He made many pictures of Mexico's peasants doing their everyday tasks. His peasants bathe, grind corn, bring bunches of creamy calla lilies to market, and bend their backs under heavy loads. Rivera painted them with rounded bodies and skin of a rich, warm brown. To see these intimate scenes is to sense the artist's love for Mexico's people.

He was at his easel in San Ángel on the morning of Saturday, May 25, 1940, painting alongside an artist named Irene Bohus, when a phone call alerted him that someone had tried to kill Trotsky the night before. Disguised as guards, a group of amateur assassins, led by the muralist David Siqueiros, a Stalinist, had entered the Trotskys' bedroom and opened fire. The couple dived behind their bed and survived — this time. Siqueiros went into hiding but was soon arrested.

Clearly, the Stalinists were still out to get Trotsky. Because Rivera had been Trotsky's ally, he feared his life was in danger too. But then he looked through a window and saw police gathering outside his house, and he knew he was also a suspect. Rivera was innocent but wanted to avoid being taken in for questioning. He claimed that Bohus sneaked him out in her car, while he crouched in the back seat under a large sheet of canvas, and helped him go into hiding. Days later, he traveled north with Paulette Goddard. They flew to Texas and from there to Los Angeles, where they parted. Goddard went to work on a motion picture, and Rivera journeyed on to San Francisco, where he stayed again in Ralph Stackpole's studio. As always, he painted; he produced ten fresco panels on the theme "Pan American Unity" as a gift for San Francisco State College.

Rivera painted these panels at the Golden Gate International Exposition. This world's fair was held on Treasure Island, in San Francisco Bay. Again he was Rivera the showman, taking part in a program called Art in Action, which invited the public to watch artists at work.

Just as the new Golden Gate and Bay Bridges arched over the water, connecting San Francisco with neighboring cities, Rivera's painting bridged the cultures of Mexico and the United States. It was "about the marriage of the artistic expression of the North and of the South of this continent," he said, the "blending of the art of the Indian, the Mexican, the Eskimo, with the kind of urge which makes the machine." Among the myriad images in the panels was a great figure, "a colossal Goddess of Life, half Indian, half machine," to symbolize the marriage of north and south. Bolted together, the panels measured seventy-four feet long and twenty-two feet high, and weighed eighty-three tons. They could be moved despite their size and weight, and this was important to Rivera, who hoped to see no more of his murals destroyed.

A sculptor named Dudley Carter was on hand and had ample time to watch Rivera at work. He saw that Rivera had assistants to prepare the fresco surface but did all the painting himself. "I remember more than once he worked all day and all night," Carter said. "If the

A tall structure known as the Tower of the Sun dominated the Golden Gate International Exhibition of 1939.

result didn't satisfy his critical eye, he would have his helpers cut off the painted area, replaster it, and he would do it all over the next day, always demanding perfection in the work." Carter, who was carving his own goddess from a redwood log twenty-six feet tall, added, "Diego Rivera was really good company. He could consume great volumes of red wine and always enjoyed himself. He was as good as a show, and helped everyone have a good time."

Rivera was in California on August 20, 1940, when back in Coyoacán, a Soviet agent named Ramón Mercader talked his way into Trotsky's study and stabbed the old revolutionary with an ice pick. Trotsky died the next day, after surgery. Rivera hired an armed guard upon hearing the news, fearing Trotsky's supporters might come after him, but no one did. The Mexican police searched his house in San Ángel, though, and they brought Frida and her sister Cristina in for questioning. The women spent two days in jail before the police determined they knew nothing about the crime and let them go. (Trotsky's staff had turned Mercader over to the authorities. He was arrested, tried, and sentenced to twenty years in prison.)

Being locked up and interrogated strained Frida's faltering health, and Dr. Leo Eloesser worried about her. He persuaded her to fly to San Francisco and put herself under his care; he also urged her to consider marrying Diego again. "Diego loves you very much, and you love him," Eloesser wrote. Diego would never be monogamous; that fact was plain. But neither had Frida been true. She had to decide whether she could accept Diego as he was—whether they could accept each other—and whether she could find fulfillment outside the relationship, in painting, keeping house, and other absorbing activities. "Reflect, dear Frida, and decide," Eloesser wrote.

Eloesser easily made Diego see that remarrying would also be good for him. Frida was not the only one who suffered; Diego missed her, and he needed her as well. Being divorced, he said, "was having a bad effect on both of us."

In San Francisco, the good doctor placed Frida in St. Luke's Hospital to help her rest.

Reunited in San Francisco, Rivera and Kahlo apply for a marriage license.

Concerned that drinking had become a habit for her, he kept her away from cognac, and her condition improved. Seeing Diego helped her feel better as well, and she talked with him about the possibility of getting married again.

Then Diego brought a friend to the hospital to meet Frida. He was Heinz Berggruen, twenty-five years old, a Jew who had fled Germany in 1936 to escape Nazi persecution. Berggruen took one look at Kahlo and was infatuated. "She was stunning, just as beautiful as in her paintings," he said. He visited her often in the hospital, and when Frida went to

New York to talk with Julien Levy about having another show of her paintings, he went too. They became lovers and spent two months together at the Barbizon-Plaza Hotel before the affair ended in arguments. They returned to California separately.

Frida went directly to Leo Eloesser's house, and on December 8, 1940, Diego's fifty-fourth birthday, she married him again in a San Francisco courtroom. This time, Frida laid down some rules: there would be no physical intimacy in this marriage; it was to be a union of two souls who loved and understood each other. Also, Frida would support herself financially, and they would share the housekeeping expenses. This kind of arrangement was less common in 1940, when a man was expected to provide for his household, than it is today. "I was so happy to have Frida back that I assented to everything," Diego confessed. As soon as the wedding ceremony was over, he went back to work on his panels for San Francisco State College.

8

PAINTED BREAD

ON APRIL 14, 1941, Guillermo Kahlo had a heart attack and died. Again Frida wept, grieving so deeply that she grew thin and ill. She wrote to Leo Eloesser about "how sweet and good he was."

The Second World War was also causing distress, for both Frida and Diego. One European country after another had surrendered to the Nazis or was occupied by force. The hateful flag of the Third Reich flew from Norway and Denmark to France and the Balkans, and Great Britain alone fought Hitler's progress. Bombs and artillery were killing soldiers and civilians and destroying art and architecture that could never be replaced. Millions of Jews and other targeted groups faced suffering and death in Nazi concentration camps. Then, on June 22, more than three million German soldiers invaded the Soviet Union. Rivera thought of the Russians he had known, especially Angelina Beloff and Marevna Vorobëv. He worried too that communism in the Soviet Union might be destroyed.

He found comfort in his growing collection of pre-Columbian figures. Over the years he had purchased thousands of these small statues, whose beauty and mystery had survived the wars and upheavals of centuries. These squat figures with strange faces spoke to Rivera about the enduring nature of art. Kahlo wrote in verse, in the diary she had begun to keep:

I have never seen tenderness as
great as Diego has
and gives when his hands
and his beautiful eyes
touch Mexican Indian sculpture.

He built a house to shelter his collection. Near Coyoacán, on a *pedregal,* a plot of rocky ground that looked like the barren landscape in some of Frida's paintings, he began a project that was big even for Diego Rivera. He oversaw the construction of a massive structure resembling an Aztec temple and built from the region's black volcanic stone. Kahlo described it rising from the landscape "like an enormous cactus, sober and elegant, strong and delicate, ancient and perennial. It shouts with the voices of centuries and days from its volcanic stone entrails: Mexico is alive!"

Rivera called the great building Anahuacalli. This Indian word means "house next to the water" as well as "house in the valley of Mexico." It can also have a poetic meaning, "house on the edge of the universe," as though space and all the heavenly bodies formed an infinite ocean. The stone mosaics Rivera designed for the walls depict images from nature and myth, like a jaguar's head and Coatlicue, the mother of the gods in Aztec lore. Inside the chambers and corridors of Anahuacalli, Rivera and Kahlo could escape the problems of the twentieth century and imagine they had traveled to Mexico's past. "I should have liked much better to have lived at that time," Rivera said. He had built the temple with an eye toward the future, though. "I return to the people the artistic heritage I was able to redeem from their ancestors," he stated. Today Anahuacalli is a museum, and Rivera's words are carved in a slab of stone that visitors see as they enter the great building.

Diego was living with Frida in Coyoacán, but husband and wife slept in separate rooms. He kept the house in San Ángel as his studio and worked there each morning. On a typical day, he returned at lunchtime to Coyoacán, where the cook always prepared plenty of creamy guacamole to spoon onto tortillas. Before eating, he popped into Frida's studio to

Rivera's shrine to pre-Columbian art, Anahuacalli, is now a museum.

see her newest paintings. After lunch, he went back to work and Frida rested. She liked to sit in the sun on her patio, and she often walked in her garden with her dogs and birds, which included not only parrots but also two turkeys and a tame eagle named Gertrude Caca Blanca (Gertrude White Poop).

At night Diego and Frida shared a snack of hot chocolate and pastries. Then, until bedtime, the two sang together, told stories, or played a game with pencils and paper called "exquisite corpse": one player drew a figure's head and shoulders, folded the sheet to hide what had been drawn, and passed it to the other. This player drew the figure's torso, folded the paper again, and handed it to the first person to draw the legs and feet. The fun came when the paper was unfolded to reveal the odd character that had been created. There were nights when Diego failed to come home, when Frida was left to worry and wonder whom he was with. Yet, the remarriage was "working well," she reported to Leo Eloesser.

She had learned, she wrote, "that *life is this way* and the rest is painted bread." Wishes are not real. An ideal marriage—the one she had hoped for—could never be.

Frida was happy keeping house in Coyoacán. She decorated the rooms with the same love of detail that she applied to dressing herself. She visited flower vendors and came home with bunches of lilies, daisies, and carnations that filled the house with color and perfume. She had the kitchen walls tiled in cheery white, yellow, and blue, and she set out jugs and bowls from the pottery markets. In the dining room, she arranged folk art on the walls and shelves and painted the floor sunshine yellow. She and Diego often lingered in this room with guests. Diego entertained with outlandish stories, and the open window let in fresh air from the garden—as well as uninvited callers. "There were monkeys jumping through the window at lunchtime. They just jumped up on the table, took some food and

Because Kahlo was an invalid and spent so much time in her bed, she decorated the nearby walls with pictures that held meaning for her.

left," remarked Ella Wolfe, wife of Rivera's friend and biographer Bertram Wolfe, who came to dine. "Nobody had a stranger household than the Riveras."

In the world outside the blue house, Kahlo's reputation as an artist continued to grow. Her work appeared in a 1941 show of modern Mexican paintings in Boston, and in a 1942 exhibition of twentieth-century portraits in New York City. In 1943, Mexico's Ministry of Education invited both Kahlo and Rivera to teach at La Esmeralda, its new school of painting and sculpture. Most of the students were young adults from needy families who paid no tuition and were given free supplies. The school building was rundown and small, with just one classroom and a patio.

Rivera was a seasoned instructor, but leading a class was a new experience for Kahlo. "Well, kids, I supposedly will be your teacher," she announced on the first day. "I have never been a teacher of painting, and I think I never will be one, because I'm always learning to paint." Instead of lecturing or showing them what to do, she guided the students as they developed their own painting styles. She led them out of the classroom and encouraged them to paint real life, up close. "We went to the streets, markets, factories, the countryside, the mountains," said one of the students, Guillermo Monroy.

Kahlo found ways for her students to share their art with the community. Some of them had studied fresco painting with Rivera, so she arranged for them to paint murals in a neighborhood *pulquería,* a shop where laborers gathered at the end of the day to drink *pulque,* an alcoholic drink made from agave, a desert plant. This *pulquería* was called La Rosita (The Little Rose), so the students put roses in the scenes of town and country life that they painted on its walls. When the murals were complete, Coyoacán held a festival in the street. Tehuana costumes were everywhere. Kahlo joined a popular folksinger, Concha Michel, to sing the peasant ballads known as *corridos.*

When Kahlo's deteriorating spine made it too tiring for her to go to La Esmeralda anymore, four dedicated students, including Guillermo Monroy, came to Coyoacán to paint in her garden. Surrounded by art, flowers, monkeys, and birds, they looked around in wonder. "It was like entering a fantasy world," recalled Arturo Estrada, another of the four. Calling themselves the Fridos, these students formed a close bond with their teacher. "Everybody loved her in a strange way," said Fanny Rabel, the only girl among the Fridos. "It was as if her life was always so close to those around her that you were tied up with her, as if you couldn't live without her." All four would go on to be successful artists.

In 1945 the Fridos painted murals in Coyoacán's public laundry, which had been built by the Mexican government to give laundresses a clean, safe place to work. The public

Today the garden at the Casa Azul, Kahlo and Rivera's blue house, looks much as it did when the artists lived there.

laundry became a refuge for these women, who were poor and often widows or single mothers. It offered rooms where they could have meals or sew, and where their children could play. The women chose the designs for the murals, which were to be pictures of them at their work. They posed while the students sketched, and they even helped pay for the project from their small earnings.

Kahlo's poor health forced her to resign from La Esmeralda in 1945, but the Fridos still came to the blue house to paint. As the pain in her spine grew steadily worse, her doctors prescribed bed rest and bound her in corsets of plaster, leather, or steel, often for months at a time. Again and again, they put her in the hospital and tried to fix her bones on the operating table. Afterward, they came up with all kinds of methods for keeping her spine straight while she healed. During one hospital stay, they hung her from a pair of rings so that her feet dangled just above the floor. A visitor found her painting at an easel while suspended this way.

Although Dr. Eloesser thought most of this surgery was unnecessary, in June 1946 Frida flew with Cristina to New York to consult a leading bone specialist and have yet another operation. Dr. Philip Wilson took a piece of bone from her hip and fused it to a section of her vertebrae, along with a steel rod. She spent eight weeks in the hospital, and after returning to Mexico she endured eight months in a steel corset, but her pain only grew worse. Frida blamed Dr. Wilson, but friends said she had defied his orders to rest and remain still. Some thought that she used her pain to keep her husband, that she feared Diego might leave if she were well enough to live on her own.

Frida painted her anguish. In a painting from this period titled *The Broken Column,* she imagined her torso split open. She depicted her spine as a marble column, the kind used by the ancient Greeks to support their temples, but this column is cracked and falling to pieces. Nails piercing Frida's flesh convey her pain, and there are tears in her eyes. Again, in a painting, she is alone in a wasteland.

At least the war was nearing its end. In December 1941, the United States had entered the conflict in response to the Japanese attack on its naval base at Pearl Harbor,

Hawaii. Many other countries had joined the fight, including Mexico, which declared war on Germany on May 22, 1942, after German submarines patrolling the Gulf of Mexico sank several of its oil tankers. The men of Esquadrón 201, a squadron of Mexican flyers known as the Aztec Eagles, distinguished themselves by helping to free the Philippines from Japanese control. In the Soviet Union, millions of soldiers and civilians had been killed or taken prisoner by Hitler's forces. But in January 1943, the hungry, exhausted "Red Army" mustered all its strength and pushed back, forcing the Germans to retreat.

On June 6, 1944, Americans and Allied forces had landed at Normandy Beach on the French coastline to liberate France and fight on into Germany. Witnessing the fall of his odious empire, Adolf Hitler committed suicide on April 30, 1945; within days, Germany surrendered. Japan announced its surrender on August 15, 1945, after U.S. planes dropped atomic bombs on the cities of Hiroshima and Nagasaki. Three months later, on November 18, 1945, crowds filled the streets of Mexico City to honor the returning Aztec Eagles.

With the world at peace, Mexico renewed its commitment to art. Diego Rivera was hired to paint a mural in the new Hotel del Prado, in Mexico City. Titled *Dream of a Sunday Afternoon in the Alameda,* it is a magical scene, a historical panorama. As in a dream, people from the past and present gather beneath the trees of the Alameda, the city park next to the hotel. Among the more than 150 people are historical figures from the time of Conquest through the Revolution. Cortés is there, his hands covered in blood. President Porfirio Díaz wears his medals and plumed hat. To the right, armed revolutionaries ride through the crowd, while to the left a pickpocket steals a handkerchief from a well-dressed gentleman whose back is turned. At the center of the mural Rivera placed himself as a mischievous schoolboy with a frog and snake escaping from his pockets. He stands next to a figure with a skull for a face, the kind drawn by the popular artist José Guadalupe Posada. Behind Diego stands Frida, a grown woman in Tehuana dress. Her hand rests on his shoulder, to show that she is his spiritual and artistic guide.

The mural presented Mexico as Rivera saw it: full of people and color, with history bearing on the present. To Rivera, there was nothing beyond the visible world. This was why he added to his fresco a banner bearing a phrase uttered in the 1800s by Ignacio Ramírez, a government official and outspoken atheist: *"Dios No Existe"* ("God does not exist").

As a child Rivera had upset his devout aunt by denouncing God and the saints in church. Now, as a grown man, he offended religious people again. The archbishop of Mexico saw the sinful words and refused to bless the new building until they were removed.

Why didn't "the archbishop bless the building and damn me?" Rivera angrily demanded. When the artist insisted the phrase would stay, outraged Catholics marched on the Hotel del Prado and tried to scratch it from the wall. The hotel's owners quieted the fury by covering the mural with red shutters.

Frida and Diego share a fond moment in 1948. Each always championed the other's work.

Plenty of people came out to protest the mural, but only a few stood up for Rivera and his work. One of them was Frida Kahlo. She sent a letter to President Miguel Alemán, who was elected in 1946, and who had been her classmate at the National Preparatory School. Censoring art, hiding it from public viewing, was a "crime against the culture of a country, against the right that every man has to express his ideas," she wrote. It was the kind of crime committed by a leader like Hitler. "If you do not act as an authentic Mexican at this critical moment," Kahlo warned, "by defending your own decrees and rights, then let the science- and history-book burnings start; let the works of art be destroyed with rocks or

In addition to his big, richly detailed murals, Rivera produced simple scenes of Mexican life.
Here he depicted an outdoor school in the countryside.

fire; let free men get kicked out of the country; let torture in, as well as prisons and concentration camps." Kahlo made an important point—that freedom is lost when good people fail to act. But President Alemán did nothing.

Diego Rivera was famous for voicing views on politics and religion that stirred up protest and debate, but for fifty years he had been enriching people's lives with his art. "Diego Rivera is one of the greatest painters of all Mexican history, and one of the few authentically great of the present epoch throughout the world," stated Carlos Chavez, director of Mexico City's Palace of Fine Arts. "The Mexican public needs to see his work—fifty years of it—all together in order to know and appreciate his stature." This was why, in 1949, the Mexican government honored Rivera by organizing a retrospective, a show featuring work from all the periods of his long artistic career. Held in the Palace of Fine Arts, this exhibition featured nearly twelve hundred works: oil paintings, watercolors, and sketches. Photographs let people see some of the frescoes Rivera had painted in other places, which were impossible to move.

Even this show caused controversy, though. The main attraction was supposed to be a new portrait of María Félix, a Mexican film star. For weeks she had been coming to Rivera's studio to pose. Because Rivera would let no one see the work-in-progress, the newspaper gossip columns were full of reports that he was painting Félix in the nude, and that the artist and actor were lovers. It turned out that Rivera had painted Félix in a sheer white dress, but she disliked the portrait and kept it out of the show. But the second rumor was true. Rivera could hardly take his eyes off the beautiful Félix.

Frida believed that this affair, like all the others, would end, and she could do little more than wait it out. María Félix had been her friend before the romance started and would remain her friend after it sputtered to its end. Meanwhile, she painted sorrowful portraits of herself, and she poured her love into her diary. "Diego: Nothing compares to your hands, to the green-gold of your eyes," she wrote on one page. On another she jotted in verse:

> *Every moment, he is my child.*
> *My newborn babe, every little while,*
> *Every day, of my own self.*

Frida used the diary to sketch her private dreams and fears. Employing the technique known as stream of consciousness, she recorded words and images as they emerged from her mind:

no moon, sun, diamond, hands—

fingertip, dot, ray, gauze, sea.

pine green, pink glass, eye,

mine, eraser, mud, mother, I am coming.

FRIDA KAHLO, *DIEGO Y YO* (*DIEGO AND I*), 1949.

Frida cries tears in this self-portrait. Again viewers can plainly see the cause of her heartache.

Mexico had paid tribute to Frida Kahlo by giving her the National Prize of Arts and Sciences in 1946, yet failing health was shrinking Frida's world. Its boundaries were often the walls of her house, and at times it was no bigger than her bedroom. Because she spent so much time in her room, Frida filled it with things that she liked to see: photographs of loved ones; dolls from her collection; folk-art skeletons sculpted from papier-mâché; and pictures of the heroes of communism, such as Chairman Mao Tse-tung of China. Still a communist in spirit, Frida rejoined the Mexican Communist Party in 1948. Diego applied for readmission too, but was rejected. The party still had not forgiven him for his government commissions and his support of Leon Trotsky.

For most of 1950, a room in Mexico City's English Hospital became Frida's world. Her back caused constant pain, and the blood circulated so poorly in her right leg that her toes were turning black. Dr. Leo Eloesser, who visited Coyoacán at the start of the year, worried about gangrene. Before going home to San Francisco, he left forty-two-year-old Frida in the care of Dr. Juan Farill, one of Mexico's leading surgeons. Between January and November, Farill and his team operated on Frida's back six times and debated whether to amputate her darkened toes. (They decided to leave them alone.) Determined to stay optimistic, Frida dressed up her hospital room with bright trinkets. Using an easel designed to rest on her bed, she painted lying down. Her sisters and friends came to see her, and she welcomed them with jokes and conversation. She invited visitors to sign a petition in support of the communist-led World Peace Council, or to help decorate the plaster casts that covered her torso between surgeries.

Stuck in the hospital, Frida missed seeing Diego receive the National Prize for Plastic Arts. (The term "plastic arts" refers to the kinds of art that can be made by molding and shaping a medium such as clay, glass, metal, or paint.) She saw her husband often, though, because he took the room next to hers, to be nearby at night. Diego's presence comforted Frida like nothing else. He read poetry to her and rocked her to sleep. About once a week he brought in a borrowed movie projector and showed her the old Laurel and Hardy films that she had laughed at in New York. If Frida seemed down, he did whatever he could think of to lighten her mood, even if he had to shake a tambourine and dance around the room, or roar like a bear with his arms raised and fingers curved like claws. The saddest nights for Frida were the ones when Diego failed to show up.

Despite the low moments, Frida declared that in the hospital she never lost her spirit. The year passed "like a fiesta," she said. "I cannot complain." She was eager to get home and do three things: paint, paint, and paint.

9

NIGHTFALL

❀

*B*ACK AT home, Frida painted a portrait of Dr. Farill. Then she made a painting of herself in her studio, seated in the wheelchair she had begun to need, beside the portrait of Dr. Farill. In this picture, her artist's palette holds a human heart instead of paint, to show that everything she put on canvas came from the deepest part of herself. She also painted still life: oranges the color of the sun; ripening bananas; and, beside the fruit, parrots and doves. As time went on, Kahlo's paintings grew softer and simpler; they lacked the fine detail of her earlier work. The painkillers she was taking made it impossible for her to paint as precisely as she once had.

Rivera was painting, as always. In 1951 he finally finished the murals he had begun in the National Palace more than twenty years before. He created a mural on the sides and bottom of a water-collection tank. In this reservoir, water from the Lerma River, Mexico's second-longest waterway, was purified. It was then piped into the homes and businesses of Mexico City. In the mural, titled *Water: Origin of Life*, he painted two great hands cradling the opening of the pipe leading into the tank, making it look as though the water were gushing through them. In the reservoir itself he painted some of the myriad life forms that depend on water, from tadpoles to humans.

He also created a movable mural for the Mexican government to display at an international peace conference in Paris. Rivera promised to paint a scene "dedicated to peace," but *The Nightmare of War and the Dream of Peace* seemed to be something else. Rivera had again contrasted life under capitalism and the ideal world he believed was possible through communism. He portrayed Mao Tse-tung and Joseph Stalin as peacemakers and

Aided by a wheelchair, Kahlo observes Rivera's mural The Nightmare of War and the Dream of Peace. *The mural has since been lost.*

the United States as the world's warmonger, the only nation to have used the atomic bomb. He showed a dying soldier hanging from a cross, and a humble Mexican laborer guiding his people toward peace.

Why did the artist who had railed against Stalin the murderer now paint him as a hero? How could the man who saw hope for the working class in Detroit's factories now depict the United States as an evil force? Rivera did these things because he was painting dishonestly. He created this mural to please the Communist Party, in the hope of being readmitted. It hurt his pride to be one of Mexico's best-known communists but rejected by the party.

This mural was "the best thing I have ever done," Rivera proudly announced, but this time it was government officials who disagreed. They refused to hang the mural, with its anti-American, pro-communist message, in Paris or anywhere. Rivera was furious, but what he did next is unclear. Somehow the mural, which measured forty feet long and ten feet high, got lost. There are stories to explain what happened to it, but they sound like legends. According to one, Rivera made a secret trip to China and gave the mural to Mao. It then hung in a Chinese government building until the Cultural Revolution of the 1960s and 1970s, when Mao ordered all examples of Western culture in China destroyed. Another story places the painting in a Moscow warehouse, where it sits to this day, crumbling and forgotten. The mural also failed to convince the Mexican Communist Party to readmit Rivera. Once more his application was turned down.

Despite the party rejecting her husband, Frida put greater faith in communism as her body weakened, just as some sick people find comfort in religion. "I am a self I am a Communist," she jotted in her diary. She loved Karl Marx, Lenin, and Mao, she wrote, and even Stalin, "as the pillars of the new Communist world." Frida never criticized Stalin as Diego had done. It is possible that, like many communists in Mexico and elsewhere, she turned a blind eye to Stalin's atrocities. These communists pointed instead to his successes, such as increased production of iron, steel, and coal. They were determined to believe that Soviet life would only improve.

Frida spent most days at home in the care of a nurse. She looked forward to visits from her sisters and friends, whose names she painted in pink on her bedroom wall. Sitting at a small table in the bedroom, these guests shared meals with their hostess. "I crave things, life, people," Frida said. Without visitors to distract her, she fell into such deep despair that, according to her nurse, at least once she tried suicide. On the rare days when she was well enough to leave the house, she went for a drive with one of her doctors or saw a movie with her nurse. Occasionally Frida and Diego went out at night with a group of friends, as they had done years earlier. It made Frida happy to sit and watch the others dance.

In 1952, a new project also brought her joy. The frescoes painted by Kahlo's students a decade before at La Rosita, the neighborhood *pulquería*, had faded and needed to be replaced. When a group of younger artists painted new murals on La Rosita's walls, Kahlo acted as their guide, advising them as they sketched. Once they started painting, she would walk to the *pulquería* on crutches to check on their progress. This time the walls would feature portraits of Rivera, Kahlo, María Félix, and other celebrities. They were being painted "for pure pleasure," Kahlo said, "for the people of Coyoacán."

The party celebrating their completion took place on December 8, 1952, Rivera's sixty-sixth birthday. In the midst of the gaiety, Kahlo tore off the corset she was wearing and shouted, "Never again!" From then on, she would be free of corsets, wheelchairs, and crutches, she vowed.

The idea that Frida Kahlo would ever walk again unaided was wishful thinking, though. In fact, when the photographer Lola Álvarez Bravo looked at Kahlo, she saw a forty-five-year-old woman near death. What a shame it would be, Bravo thought, if this great artist were to die without having a one-woman show in Mexico. Kahlo had been the subject of a solo exhibition at the Julien Levy Gallery in New York, but never in her own country, and Bravo was going to change that. She offered to host the event at her Gallery of Contemporary Art, in Mexico City.

The show would include more than thirty paintings and twenty drawings, the work of two decades. Kahlo was jubilant and made the invitations herself, from colored paper and yarn. On them she copied lines of poetry that she had composed:

> *With friendship and love*
> *born of the heart*
> *I am pleased to invite you*
> *to my humble exhibition . . .*

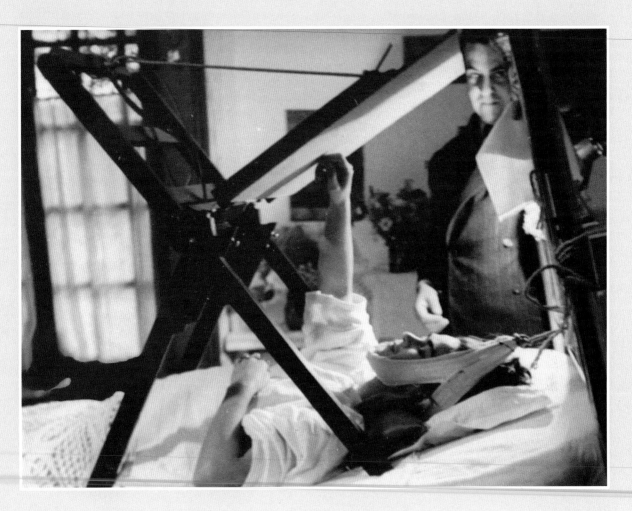

A custom-built easel allows Kahlo to paint while in traction.

People knew Kahlo was ill, but they were keen to see the artist as well as her art. Bravo's telephone rang day and night as art lovers and reporters called to ask if Kahlo would attend the opening on April 13. Kahlo dearly hoped to be there, but as the date drew near, it looked as though she might have to miss the momentous event. Her doctors had ordered her to remain lying down and not to move.

Then Kahlo had a brainstorm: Why not attend the opening lying down? She hired workers to move her hefty four-poster bed to Bravo's gallery, where it stood among the paintings as if part of the show. It was there for her on opening day, when she rode in an ambulance to the gallery on busy Amberes Street. Medical workers carried her on a stretcher into the packed gallery and, as people moved aside, laid her on the waiting bed. There, as dazzling as ever, Kahlo greeted one by one the friends and admirers who had come to see her and her work. Important people from the Mexican art world, from Dr. Atl to José Clemente Orozco, were on hand. For Rivera, his wife's show was the brightest moment of 1953. "Even I was impressed when I saw all her work together," he admitted. The folksinger Concha Michel came too, and until the early hours of morning, she and Kahlo led the crowd in song:

Child of my heart,
Tomorrow is another day.

It was a night never to forget, but Frida's friends noticed a change in her. She laughed and sang as always, but part of her seemed far away. Rivera understood why only later, when he said, "She must have realized she was bidding good-bye to life."

"I am not sick," Frida insisted. "I am broken." Sick or broken—it hardly mattered. The pain in her leg was becoming more than anyone could bear. Even at very high doses, pain-killers no longer helped. By August, gangrene had set in; there was no doubt any longer. Dr. Farill told Frida the leg would have to come off. Frida let out a wail, a gut-wrenching cry of the deepest dejection. "I am DISINTEGRATION," she wrote in her diary, and she drew herself as a soiled, discarded doll missing its leg. In a courageous moment she noted, "Feet what do I need them for if I have wings to fly."

Frida tried to be strong, but when Dr. Farill and his team amputated her right leg at the knee they took her spirit with it. "Night is falling in my life," she confided to a friend. Diego thought she had lost the will to live, and a psychiatrist confirmed this. After she went home, her wounded limb healed, and in time she learned to walk on an artificial leg. She had a pair of fancy boots made, of red leather with gold embroidery, to make her feet look pretty.

She had spells of hysterical crying, though, when no one but Diego could calm her. He would tell her stories, read and sing to her, or simply hold her until she relaxed enough to fall asleep. Once each crisis was over, he hurried to San Ángel, to make up for the time at his easel that he had missed. Diego had to push himself to comfort Frida, because nurturing never came naturally to him. Frida's suffering frequently brought him to tears and sometimes kept him away from the blue house for days.

Nearly a year passed before Frida Kahlo did more with paint than dabble. She worked in her studio in Coyoacán, her spine held straight by a sash that tied her torso to the wheelchair. When painting in this position grew too tiring and painful, she worked in bed. One day she painted watermelons, round and ripe and lying on the earth against a sky tinged with purple. On the juicy, red flesh of a melon slice she painted the words *"Viva la vida"* ("Long live life"). This was the last picture she would ever paint.

She left the house on July 2, 1954, although ill with pneumonia, to attend a rally with Diego. On this unseasonably cold, damp day, communists and others were protesting the role played by the U.S. Central Intelligence Agency (CIA) in a recent coup d'état in Guatemala. A land-reform program put in place by Guatemalan president Jacobo Árbenz Guzmán had threatened the holdings—and the profits—of the United Fruit Company, a U.S. corporation that was Guatemala's largest landowner. Acting on orders from higher up, the CIA helped the Guatemalan army force Árbenz out of office. Árbenz resigned on June

27, 1954, and took refuge in the Mexican Embassy. It was no surprise that the new regime, led by General Carlos Castillo Armas, promised to be friendlier to U.S. interests.

The woman Diego pushed in her wheelchair that day looked haggard and ill. Taking part in the demonstration worsened her pneumonia, yet four days later Frida was in her dining room to greet the hundred or so friends who stopped by to wish her happiness as she turned forty-seven. Each friend went away well fed, having feasted on turkey *mole,* a rich stew made with chilis, tomatoes, and chocolate. The happy day ended in Frida's bedroom, where she continued to welcome guests until after eight o'clock.

Frida's birthday passed, and another important date drew near. August 21 would be the twenty-fifth anniversary of the day when she and Diego first wed. She had a present for her husband, a ring, but she gave it to him early, on the evening of July 12, and told him she wanted to say goodbye. That night her fever rose and she strained to breathe, but at last she fell asleep. When her nurse checked on her the next morning, she was dead. She had made a final entry in her diary: "I hope the leaving is joyful—and I hope never to return."

Her friends dressed Frida's body in a black Tehuana skirt, white *huipil,* and jewelry. They braided her hair with flowers and ribbons and laid her out on her bed. Later that day, the body was moved to the lobby of the National Institute of Fine Arts, so all of Mexico could honor the beloved artist who found inspiration in her homeland. Diego Rivera stood beside the gray coffin, heartbroken and lost. The adolescent girl who targeted him with her pranks, the young woman who showed him her paintings and won his love, the vibrant figure whose colorful personal style made her one of a kind, the wife who embraced joy and lived in pain, the artist who transformed her suffering into lasting beauty: she was forever gone.

The director of the institute, a writer named Andrés Iduarte, was another of Kahlo's old schoolmates. He had given permission for her body to lie in state only after Rivera promised to keep politics out of the event. But when one of Kahlo's students draped her coffin in a communist flag, Rivera refused to take it off. He would sooner stand with Frida's body out in the street, he declared. He was saved from making good on this threat by former president Lázaro Cárdenas, the man who had invited Trotsky to Mexico, who proudly took a place in Kahlo's honor guard despite the crimson flag. (Iduarte would later be fired for failing to make Rivera remove it.)

In the early afternoon of July 14, as a hearse carried Kahlo's remains from the Palace of Fine Arts to the crematorium, five hundred mourners followed on foot. Family members, friends, artists, writers, dignitaries, and communists: they packed themselves into the small crematorium or stood outside, getting wet in the rain. They listened as Andrés Iduarte delivered a moving eulogy. "The brilliant and strong-willed creature that in our day lit the classrooms of the National Preparatory School has died," he said. "An extraordinary artist has died." To Iduarte, Kahlo was an "awakened spirit, a generous heart, sensitivity in the flesh, a lover of art even to the point of death." He lamented, *"Ha muerto Frida."* Frida has died.

10

THE GREAT FIESTA

*F*RIDA DIED, and Diego grew old in an instant. His face sagged and turned ashen, and his shoulders dropped. He came to a sad understanding. "Too late now," he said, "I realized that the most wonderful part of my life had been my love for Frida."

In September 1954, he was at last readmitted to the Communist Party of Mexico; soon afterward, he gave the blue house in Coyoacán and his temple filled with pre-Columbian art, Anahuacalli, to the Mexican government. They would be preserved as museums where future generations could learn about Kahlo, Rivera, and the art of Mexico's past.

Despite his deep grief for Frida, on July 29, 1955, a little more than a year after her death, Diego married again. His new wife, Emma Hurtado, was an old friend, an art dealer he had worked with since 1946. Within months of the wedding, however, Diego learned he had cancer. He journeyed with Emma to Moscow for treatments with radioactive cobalt, a therapy not yet available in Mexico. Seven months later the Soviet doctors pronounced him cured. Before returning to Mexico, he and Emma toured Czechoslovakia, East Germany, and Poland, countries that had come under Soviet control after World War II.

The events of the previous two years—Frida's death, his remarriage, and his illness—caused Rivera to reflect on his beliefs and reconsider his strongly held views. One day in 1956, he surprised the Mexican public by returning to the Hotel del Prado and painting over the controversial words *Dios No Existe* on his shuttered mural. Explaining his action, he simply said, "I am a Catholic."

Like his murals, Rivera was a national treasure. In December 1956, on his seventieth birthday, the city of Guanajuato honored him with a banquet. City officials placed a marker on the house where Rivera was born in 1886. Accompanying the great artist as he returned to his first home were Emma, his wife; María, his sister; and Lupe and Ruth, his daughters with his first wife, Lupe Marín. Lupe had raised her girls to be accomplished women. Guadalupe Rivera Marín was a writer and lawyer who would serve as Mexico's ambassador to Italy, and Ruth Rivera Marín was an architect. Rivera had supported them financially while they were growing up, but he had spent little time with them.

Rivera's daughter with Marevna Vorobëv, Marika, grew up to be a dancer and actor. She used the last name Rivera and identified herself as the Mexican artist's daughter. For many years Marika sent her father letters and

Late in life Rivera continued to find pleasure at Anahuacalli, surrounded by his pre-Columbian art.

photographs of herself in the hope of having a relationship with him. But, "I never responded," Rivera wrote. "The past was the past."

Nine months after the celebration in Guanajuato, in September 1957, Rivera suffered a stroke. A blood clot lodged in a vessel feeding his brain, paralyzing his right arm. But he was an artist to the end, so he kept on working with his left hand. He completed a series of mosaic murals on the stone walls surrounding the Acapulco home of Dolores Olmedo, a woman who had modeled for him in the 1930s. These brightly tiled walls portray ancient Mexican gods, including the feathered serpent Quetzalcóatl, with his many-colored plumes. Rivera and Emma Hurtado were staying with Dolores Olmedo on November 24, when a heart attack ended the artist's life.

Rivera had asked to have his ashes mixed with Kahlo's, but Mexico's president arranged instead for them to be placed in the Rotunda of Illustrious Persons in Mexico City. There they rest near the remains of presidents, military leaders, writers, artists, and other distinguished Mexicans.

No other painter, in any epoch, had done work as rich or as varied as Rivera's, observed Dr. Atl, who was an old man of eighty-one when Diego Rivera died. For Dr. Atl, confronting Rivera's paintings was like standing before the sea. "The first thing that strikes us is the enormity—the oceanic immensity," he said. "Thousands and thousands of square meters painted on the walls of ancient chapels, in the unending corridors of public buildings, in palace stairwells, in laboratories and schools. In addition, thousands of paintings and drawings came out of his workshop—portraits, compositions, and landscapes—and are scattered on five continents."

Frida Kahlo once said that her husband imagined an ideal world. It was "a great fiesta in which each and every being takes part," she explained. It was "a fiesta of form, of color, of movement, of sound."

La forma. El color. El movimiento. El sonido.

This great fiesta, this ideal world, was the one he painted, and Frida was "the center of

Frida y Diego vivieron en esta casa (Frida and Diego lived in this house),
1929–1954: *words painted on a wall at Casa Azul, the blue house in Coyoacán.*

all," Diego wrote. She was "in the earth and in matter, thunder, lightning and the light rays."

She was "the mother-sea, tempest, nebula, woman."

El tempestad. La nebulosa. La mujer.

Adiós.

Actors Salma Hayek and Alfred Molina portrayed Frida Kahlo and Diego Rivera in the 2002 film Frida.

Paintings by

❀

Frida Kahlo
&
Diego Rivera

Diego Rivera painted many simple scenes of Mexican life, but he is remembered best for his big, boisterous, crowded murals. Like Hollywood epics of the past, Rivera's frescoes often feature a "cast of thousands." For Rivera, being an artist was like leaning out a wide window and turning to the right and left so his eyes might absorb every detail of the busy world he would paint on walls and canvases. "Diego was a deluge of work," the Latin American art critic Raquel Tibol has said. "So many cultural themes opened his interest in a very vibrant way."

For Frida Kahlo, being an artist was like looking in a mirror. Her highly original self-portraits reflect feelings and ideas drawn from deep within herself. Her paintings enthrall and sometimes shock viewers with their intimacy. "Kahlo's self-portraits are remarkable in that they gave visibility to events and emotions that had rarely, if ever, been represented in, much less acknowledged as legitimate subjects for, art," art historian Sarah M. Lowe has written.

More than half a century after their deaths, Rivera and Kahlo remain two of the most important artists of the twentieth century, although for many years Rivera's reputation overshadowed Kahlo's. Her work began attracting more attention in the 1970s as the feminist movement gained momentum. At that time viewers found in Kahlo's self-portraits something that was missing from most of the paintings they saw: a frank depiction of a woman's inner life.

A number of museums in the United States and Mexico own works by Kahlo and Rivera. Not only do the museums display the paintings on their walls, but they often make them available online as well. Some of these museums are listed here.

The United States

Albright-Knox Art Gallery, Buffalo, New York
www.albrightknox.org

Detroit Institute of Arts, Detroit, Michigan
www.dia.org

Harry Ransom Center at the University of Texas, Austin, Texas
www.hrc.utexas.edu

Los Angeles County Museum of Art, Los Angeles, California
www.lacma.org

Madison Museum of Contemporary Art, Madison, Wisconsin
www.mmoca.org

Metropolitan Museum of Art, New York, New York
www.metmuseum.org

Museum of Fine Arts, Boston, Massachusetts
www.mfa.org

Museum of Modern Art, New York, New York
www.moma.org

National Museum of Women in the Arts, Washington, D.C.
www.nmwa.org

Phoenix Art Museum, Phoenix, Arizona
www.phxart.org

San Francisco Museum of Modern Art, San Francisco, California
www.sfmoma.org

Mexico

Museo Casa Diego Rivera (Diego Rivera Birthplace), Guanajuato

Museo Casa Estudio Diego Rivera (The Diego Rivera House and Studio), Mexico City
www.estudiodiegorivera.bellasartes.gob.mx

Museo Dolores Olmedo (Dolores Olmedo Museum), Xochimilco, Mexico City
www.museodoloresolmedo.org.mx

Museo Diego Rivera Anahuacalli (The Diego Rivera Museum at Anahuacalli), Coyoacán
www.museoanahuacalli.org.mx/framesetenglish.htm

Museo Frida Kahlo (Frida Kahlo Museum), Coyoacán
www.museofridakahlo.org.mx

Museo Mural Diego Rivera (Diego Rivera Mural Museum), Mexico City
www.museomuraldiegorivera.bellasartes.gob.mx

Another way to enjoy the art of Frida Kahlo and Diego Rivera

is through books such as these:

Diego Rivera, by Pete Hamill
New York: Harry N. Abrams, 1999

Diego Rivera: The Cubist Portraits, 1913–1917, by Sylvia Navarete
London: Philip Wilson, 2009

Diego Rivera: Murals for the Museum of Modern Art, by Leah Dickerman and Anna Indych-López
New York: Museum of Modern Art, 2011

Frida Kahlo, edited by Emma Dexter and Tanya Barson
London: Tate Publishing, 2005

Frida Kahlo, 1907–1954: Pain and Passion, by Andrea Kettenmann
New York: Barnes and Noble Books, 2004

Frida Kahlo: The Paintings, by Hayden Herrera
New York: HarperPerrennial, 2002

Paintings by

Frida Kahlo

Retrato de Alicia Galant (Portrait of Alicia Galant), 1927
A friend named Alicia Galant posed for one of Frida Kahlo's early portraits.

Frieda and Diego Rivera, 1931

Kahlo commemorated her marriage to Rivera in this work. For a few years she used the traditional German spelling of her name, Frieda, to acknowledge her father's roots in Germany. She had been baptized Frida, however.

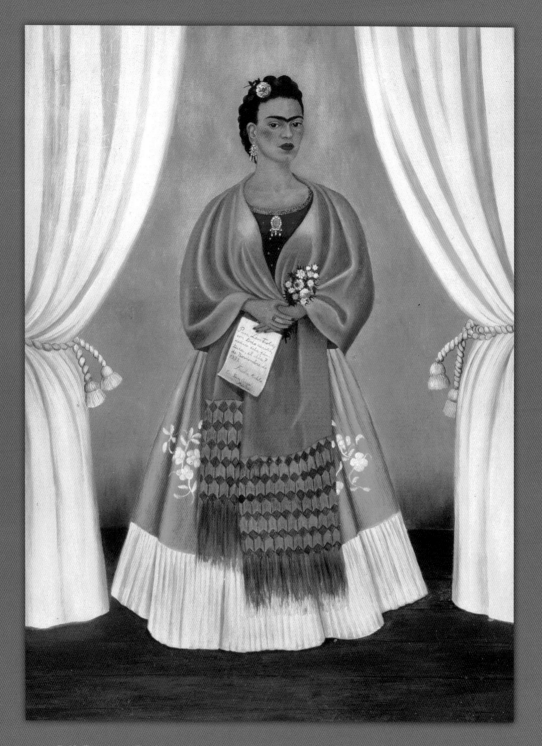

Self-Portrait Dedicated to Leon Trotsky, 1937, 30 x 24 in., oil on Masonite.
The artist gave this self-portrait to Leon Trotsky at the close of their brief love affair.
In the painting she holds a dedication stating that it was presented "with all love."

Self-Portrait with Necklace of Thorns, 1940

Kahlo explored her feelings in many self-portraits like this one. The thorns circling her neck are a symbol of suffering, but what does the dead hummingbird mean? And the fairylike insects flying above her head—might they be hopes or dreams?

The Little Deer, 1946

Kahlo's pet deer, Granizo, served as a model for this work. The painter imagines herself as a wounded stag in a barren forest. Could the arrows running along her back stand for the pain she suffered from her damaged spine? Or could they be another kind of pain?

Still Life with Parrot, 1951
The fine detail and careful brushwork of earlier paintings are missing
from Kahlo's late efforts.

Paintings by

Diego Rivera

No. 9, Nature Morte Espagnole, 1915
In this Cubist work, Rivera depicted a ceramic jug and other objects arranged on
a wooden tabletop in Spain.

Día de flores (Flower Day), 1925
A peasant sets out to carry a harvest of calla lilies to market in this scene of rural Mexican life.

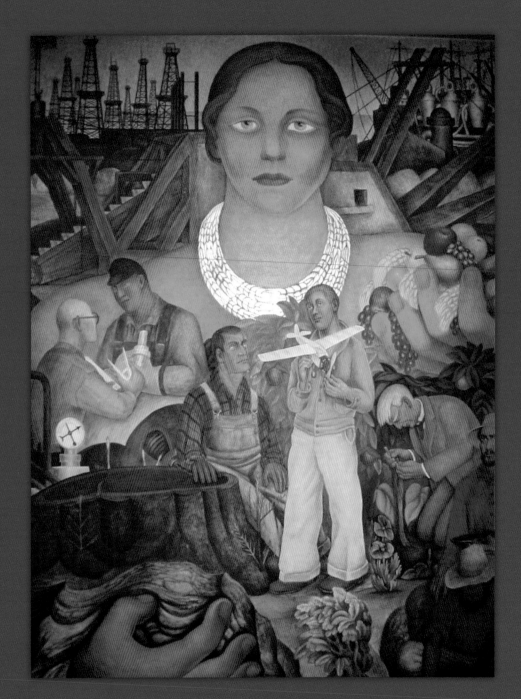

Allegory of California, 1931

A female figure embraces the wealth of California—its bountiful crops, its history, and its scientific progress—in the mural Rivera painted for the San Francisco Stock Exchange.

Detroit Industry (north wall), 1932–1933

In the main panel on this wall in the Detroit Institute of Arts, workers lift, haul, and solder to build engines and transmissions for Ford automobiles. Some people objected to the upper-right panel, showing a child being vaccinated, for its similarity to paintings of the Nativity.

Danza en Tehuantepec (Dance in Tehuantepec), 1935
Rivera captured the grace of these Mexican dancers.

Pan American Unity (panel 2), 1940

So much is happening in this section of the mural Rivera painted for the Golden Gate Exhibition! A graceful diver floats through the air while, behind her, boats sail in and out of San Francisco Bay. An artist carving a serpent's head seems to draw on Mexico's past. Frida Kahlo poses at her easel near heroes from history, subjects of a mural in progress. It is even possible to spot Rivera himself at work.

Frida Kahlo & Diego Rivera

❀

A Timeline

1886

December 8:   Diego Rivera and his twin brother, Carlos, are born in Guanajuato, Mexico.

1888   Rivera's twin brother dies.

1892   The Riveras move to Mexico City.

1896   Rivera begins studying art at the San Carlos Academy.

1906   Rivera graduates from the San Carlos Academy.

1907   Rivera arrives in Spain to study painting with Eduardo Chicharro, with support from the government of Veracruz.

July 6:   Frida Kahlo is born in Coyoacán, a suburb of Mexico City.

1909   Rivera begins travels that will take him to Paris, Bruges, and London.

   In Bruges, Rivera meets Russian artist Angelina Beloff.

1910   Rivera sails to Mexico for an October show of his paintings.

   President Porfirio Díaz defeats Francisco Madero in a rigged vote; this election outcome sets in motion events leading to the Mexican Revolution.

1911	Rivera and Beloff begin living together in the Montparnasse section of Paris.
	Rivera explores Cubism.
February:	Madero leads an attack on the Mexican town of Casas Grandes; the revolution begins.
May 25:	President Díaz steps down.
1914	Rivera meets Pablo Picasso.
April:	A Paris gallery exhibits Rivera's Cubist paintings.
June 28:	The assassination of Archduke Franz Ferdinand of Austria-Hungary leads to declarations of war in Europe.
	Kahlo contracts polio.
1916	Rivera begins a second romantic relationship with Russian artist Marevna Vorobëv.
August 11:	Rivera and Beloff's son, Diego María, is born.
1917	
October 28:	Fourteen-month-old Diego María dies.
1918	
November 11:	The armistice ending World War I is signed.
1919	Vorobëv gives birth to a daughter, Marika, whom Rivera refuses to acknowledge.
1920–21	Having abandoned Cubism and in search of a new painting style, Rivera tours Italy.
1921	
July:	Rivera sails home to Mexico.

1921 (cont.)	Rivera's father, Don Diego Rivera, dies.
1922	Kahlo enrolls in Mexico City's National Preparatory School.
	Rivera paints a mural at the National Preparatory School and first encounters Kahlo. He now draws inspiration from Mexican artistic traditions.
June:	Rivera marries Guadalupe Marín.
1923	Rivera's mother, María del Pilar, dies.
	Rivera begins painting murals in the Ministry of Education.
1924	Rivera and Marín's daughter Guadalupe is born.
1925	
September 17:	Kahlo suffers catastrophic injuries while riding a bus that collides with a streetcar; she learns to paint while recovering.
1926	Rivera begins painting murals in the former chapel at Chapingo.
1927	Rivera and Marín's daughter Ruth is born.
	Rivera begins an affair with model and photographer Tina Modotti that destroys his marriage.
	Rivera travels to the Soviet Union for the tenth anniversary of the Russian Revolution.
	Kahlo joins the Communist Party.
1928	Kahlo and Rivera meet again.
1929	
April:	Rivera is appointed director of the San Carlos Academy.
August 21:	Kahlo and Rivera marry.

1929 (cont.)	Rivera is expelled from the Communist Party.
	U.S. ambassador Dwight Morrow commissions Rivera to paint murals in the Palace of Cortés, Cuernavaca.
	Kahlo undergoes an abortion.
1930	
November:	Rivera and Kahlo go to San Francisco, where he paints murals in the California School of Fine Arts and the city's stock exchange.
December:	Kahlo befriends Leo Eloesser, M.D.
1931	The San Francisco Society of Women Artists includes Kahlo's painting *Frieda and Diego Rivera* in its annual show.
	The Museum of Modern Art in New York hosts a solo exhibition of Rivera's work.
1932	Rivera paints twenty-seven panels in the Detroit Institute of Arts.
July:	Kahlo suffers a miscarriage requiring thirteen days of hospitalization. The experience leads her to paint *Henry Ford Hospital* and other personal, symbolic works.
September 15:	Kahlo's mother, Matilde Calderón, dies.
1933	Commissioned by the powerful Rockefeller family, Rivera begins a mural in the RCA Building in New York City titled *Man at the Crossroads*.
May 9:	The Rockefellers fire Rivera after he refuses to remove the face of Vladimir Lenin from his mural.
December 20:	Rivera and Kahlo sail home to Mexico.
1934	Rivera's unfinished mural in the RCA Building is destroyed.
	Kahlo and Rivera move into their new houses in San Ángel.
	Rivera begins an affair with Kahlo's sister Cristina.

1935	Kahlo paints *A Few Small Nips*. She moves out of her house in San Ángel and into an apartment in Mexico City.
1937	
January 9:	The exiled Leon Trotsky arrives in Mexico with his wife; the couple takes up residence in the Kahlo house in Coyoacán.
	Kahlo and Trotsky have a brief affair.
November 7:	Kahlo presents Trotsky with a self-portrait.
1938	Kahlo's paintings from this year include *What the Water Gave Me* and *The Suicide of Dorothy Hale*.
	Paintings by Kahlo appear in a group show in Mexico City.
November 1:	Art dealer Julien Levy exhibits Kahlo's work at his New York gallery.
	Kahlo has an affair with photographer Nickolas Muray.
1939	
January:	Kahlo sails for France to attend a Paris show of her work.
April:	The Trotskys move out of the Coyoacán house.
November 6:	Kahlo and Rivera divorce.
	Kahlo paints *The Two Fridas* and other works.
1940	Rivera paints ten frescoes collectively titled *Pan American Unity* at the Golden Gate International Exposition, San Francisco.
August 21:	A Soviet agent assassinates Trotsky.
December 8:	Kahlo and Rivera remarry.
1941	Rivera builds Anahuacalli, a temple to house his pre-Columbian art.
	Kahlo's art is exhibited in Boston.

1942	Several of Kahlo's portraits are part of a show in New York City.
1943	Kahlo and Rivera begin teaching at La Esmeralda, a new government-sponsored art school.
1945	Ill health forces Kahlo to resign from La Esmeralda, although she continues to mentor several students.
1946	Kahlo receives the National Prize of Arts and Sciences.
June:	Kahlo flies to New York for spinal surgery.
	Kahlo paints *The Broken Column*.
1947	Rivera begins the mural *Dream of a Sunday Afternoon in the Alameda* in the Hotel del Prado in Mexico City.
1948	Kahlo rejoins the Communist Party.
1949	The Mexican government honors Rivera with a retrospective show of his work.
	Rivera romances film star María Felíx.
1950	Kahlo spends much of the year in Mexico City's English Hospital.
	Rivera receives the National Prize for Plastic Arts.
1951	Rivera completes his work at the National Palace.
1952	Rivera paints *The Nightmare of War and the Dream of Peace*. This mural will be lost.
1953	
April 13:	Kahlo attends the opening of her show at the Gallery of Contemporary Art in Mexico City in her bed.
	Kahlo's right leg is amputated below the knee.

1954	Kahlo paints her final work, *Viva la vida*.
July 2:	Kahlo and Rivera demonstrate against U.S. involvement in Guatemalan politics.
July 13:	Kahlo dies.
September:	Rivera is readmitted to the Communist Party.

1955	
July 29:	Rivera marries Emma Hurtado.
	Rivera travels with Hurtado to Moscow for cancer treatment.

1956	Rivera and Hurtado tour communist countries in eastern Europe.
	Rivera's birthplace, Guanajuato, honors him with a banquet.

1957	Rivera creates mosaic murals at the home of Dolores Olmedo.
September:	Rivera suffers a stroke.
November 24:	Rivera dies of a heart attack.

Notes

·············· ❀ ··············

1. The Artists Wed

1 Kahlo, "On guard, Diego . . ." is quoted in Rivera and March, p. 75.

2 Kahlo, "Would it cause you any annoyance . . ." is quoted in Rivera and March, p. 76.

   Rivera, "I had no idea . . ." is from Rivera and March, p. 76.

3 Kahlo, "*¡Diego, baje!*" is quoted in Bambi, June 13, 1954, p. 6C.

   Rivera, "fine nervous body . . ." is from Rivera and March, p. 102.

4 Kahlo, "Look, I have not come . . ." is quoted in Bambi, June 13, 1954, p. 6C.

   Rivera, "a vital sensuality . . ." and "In my opinion . . ." are from Rivera and March, p. 103.

   Kahlo, "Yes, so what? . . ." is quoted in Rivera and March, p. 103.

   Rivera, "Frida had already become . . ." is from Rivera and March, p. 104.

   "It was like a marriage . . ." is quoted in Bambi, June 13, 1954, p. 6C.

   Guillermo Kahlo, "Note well, my daughter . . ." is quoted in Bambi, June 13, 1954, p. 6C.

5 "was celebrated in a very cordial atmosphere . . ." is quoted in Herrera 1983, p. 99.

6 Marín, "You see these two sticks? . . ." is quoted in Wolfe 2000, p. 249.

   Rivera, "an artist who tore open her chest . . ." is from Rivera 1968, p. 10.

7 Kahlo, "the eternally curious one . . ." is from Museo Nacional de Artes Plásticas, p. 41.

2. The Curious One

8   "quaint old mining town" is from Smith, p. 7.

Martha, "She can hear me!" is quoted in Marnham, p. 19.

13   Rebull, "These things which we call pictures . . ." is quoted in Wolfe 2000, p. 33.

14   Rivera, "Best of all . . ." is from Rivera and March, p. 20.

15   Murillo (Dr. Atl), "The great mural painters! . . ." is quoted in Sáenz, p. 81.

16   Chicharro, "astonishing progress . . ." is quoted in Marnham, p. 58.

17   Pompey, "María was cultured . . ." is quoted in Campoy, p. 157.

18   Rivera, "To Mademoiselle Angelina Beloff . . ." is quoted in Rivera, Marín, and Rivera, p. 68.

19   Rivera, "my beloved wife . . ." is quoted in Rivera, Marín, and Rivera, p. 68.

"a very great artist," is from Moyssén, p. 458.

"an artistic spectacle . . ." is from Moyssén, p. 462.

20   Rivera, "I could not remain . . ." is quoted in Rivera, Marín, and Rivera, p. 80.

21   Díaz, "If the Fatherland . . ." is quoted in Beals, p. 450

3. An Accidental Artist

22   Kahlo, "like a little bell . . ." is from Tibol 1977, p. 20.

24   Kahlo, "My toys were those of a boy . . ." is from Tibol 1977, p. 28.

25   Gómez Arias, "had a fresh, perhaps ingenuous . . ." is quoted in Herrera 1983, p. 33.

26   Kahlo, "Just imagine, my poor little mother . . ." is from Tibol 2003, p. 31.

Kahlo, "In this hospital . . ." is quoted in Herrera 1983, p. 50.

28   Calles, "The hour is approaching . . ." is quoted in Mayer, p. 44.

4. Reborn

30   Apollinaire, "Subject-matter now counts . . ." is from Apollinaire, pp. 11–12.

     Rivera, "Everything about the movement . . ." is from Rivera and March, p. 58.

31   Rivera, "Will and energy blazed . . ." is from Rivera and March, p. 60.

32   Rivera, "[We felt] as remote from the conflict . . ." is from Rivera and March, p. 62.

34   Rivera, "daughter of the Armistice" is quoted in Wolfe 2000, p. 104.

35   Faure, "the most important phenomenon . . ." is from Faure, p. 4.

     Faure, "laid the foundations . . ." and "made possible, in fact . . ." are from Faure, p. 5.

     Vorobëv, "I still hoped . . ." is from Vorobëv, p. 263.

36   Rivera, "All the colors . . ." and "I am reborn" are from Rivera and March, p. 72.

     Vasconcelos, "was to put the public in contact . . ." is quoted in Rochfort, p. 21.

37   Vorobëv, "Perhaps he thought . . ." is from Vorobëv, p. 264.

     Rivera, "Lupe was a beautiful, spirited animal" is from Rivera and March, p. 83.

38   *To open paths* . . . is quoted in Wolfe 2000, p. 153.

39   Bynner, "Where could one meet a jollier, heartier giant . . ." is from Bynner, p. 28.

40   Eloesser, "He regaled me during several days . . ." is from Shumacker, p. 235.

     Eloesser, "he worked on the walls . . ." is from Shumacker, p. 233.

5. South and North of the Border Line

44   Kahlo, "the City of the World" is quoted in Rivera and March, p. 106.

45   Rivera, "I was almost frightened . . ." is from Rivera and March, p. 106.

     Kahlo, "I've never seen more beautiful children . . ." is from Zamora, p. 40.

     Weston, "He took me clear off my feet . . ." is from Newhall, p. 198.

47 Eloesser, "a girl of unusual beauty . . ." is from Shumacker, pp. 235–36.

Eloesser, "Never did a painter . . ." is from Shumacker, p. 236.

Callahan, "If it is a joke . . ." is quoted in Wolfe 2000, p. 292.

48 O'Gorman, "caused a sensation . . ." is quoted in *Las casas de Juan O'Gorman,* p. 30.

50 Kahlo, "I feel rage . . ." and "an enormous, dirty chicken coop" are from *Querido Doctorcito,* p. 98.

Kahlo, "I hate you" is quoted in Thomas, p. 422.

Rivera, "the great saga . . ." is quoted in Davies, January 19, 1933, p. 4.

50–51 Kahlo, "I don't like it . . ." and "I am now *two* months pregnant" are from *Querido Doctorcito,* p. 109.

51 Kahlo, "What I want to know . . ." is from *Querido Doctorcito,* p. 110.

52 Kahlo, "tells me I can't do this . . ." is quoted in Herrera 1983, p. 141.

Rivera, "as beautiful as the masterpieces . . ." is from Rivera, April 1933, p. 291.

Bloch, "She looked so tiny . . ." is quoted in Herrera 1983, p. 141.

53 Rivera, "You are not dealing . . ." is quoted in Herrera 1983, p. 142.

53–54 "She has acquired . . ." is from Davies, February 2, 1933, p. 16.

54 Rivera, "the way that we have clung . . ." is quoted in Davies, January 19, 1933, p. 4.

Rivera, *"horrorosa"* is from Wolfe 2000, p. 304.

55 Bloch, "The last hours . . ." is quoted in Herrera 1983, p. 154.

Bloch, "cries and cries . . ." is quoted in Herrera 1983, p. 155.

Kahlo, "Everything without you . . ." and Rivera, "I am very sad here . . ." are quoted in Herrera 1983, p. 155.

56 Kahlo, "I can work . . ." is quoted in Herrera 1983, p. 156.

Kahlo, "What I did . . ." and "Mr. Ford, are you Jewish?" are quoted in Herrera 1983, p. 135.

"anti-American," and "Communistic," are quoted in Marnham, p. 244.

57 Rivera, "the pictorial representation . . ." is from Rivera, April 1933, p. 295.

6. Wounds

58 Ford, "I admire Rivera's spirit . . ." is quoted in Wolfe 2000, p. 314.

60 "Rivera Paints Scenes . . ." and "waves of red headdress . . ." are from Lilly, p. 3.

61 Rockefeller, "seriously offend . . ." is quoted in *New York Herald Tribune*.

62 Rivera, "a figure of some great American historical leader . . ." is quoted in Wolfe 2000, p. 327.

Rivera, "should prefer the physical destruction . . ." is quoted in Wolfe 2000, p. 326.

"Freedom in art!" is quoted in Herrera 1983, p. 165.

"Save Rivera's painting!" is quoted in *Time*, May 22, 1933.

"the uncompleted fresco . . ." is quoted in Colby, p. 60.

Rivera, "the property of all humanity . . ." is quoted in Wolfe 2000, p. 331.

63 Rivera, "the best that I have painted" is from Rivera 1934, p. 31.

64 Nevelson, "All were treated like one body . . ." is from Nevelson, p. 57.

Rivera, "I, unfortunately, was not a faithful husband . . ." is from Rivera and March, p. 83.

Nevelson, "If a man's a genius . . ." is quoted in Lisle, p. 94.

Bloch, "too perfect a person . . ." is quoted in Herrera 1983, p. 170.

65 Rivera, "The buildings which today have been erected . . ." is from Rivera 1934, p. 16.

66 Nevelson, "I had my future . . ." is quoted in Lisle, p. 98.

67 Eaton, "I had to balance . . ." is quoted in Herrera 1983, p. 196.

Kahlo, "It costs me very dearly . . ." is from Tibol 1999, p. 188.

68 "It was just a few . . ." is from Kettenmann, p. 39.

69 Kahlo, "I cannot love him . . ." is quoted in Wolfe 2000, p. 396.

Rivera, "If I loved a woman . . ." is from Rivera and March, p. 180.

70 Rivera, "the Undertaker of the Revolution" is from Rivera, May 1940, p. 114.

OUT WITH TROTSKY . . . is quoted in Patenaude, p. 30.

Natalia Trotsky, "We were on a new planet . . ." is quoted in Carmichael, p. 432.

70–71 Leon Trotsky, "Do you wish to see . . ." is from Trotsky, p. 7.

72 Farrell, "one of the saddest faces . . ." is quoted in Patenaude, p. 61.

Farrell, "an extremely fertile and quick mind . . ." is quoted in Landers, p. 197.

Trotsky, "composed of falsifiers . . ." is quoted in Landers, p. 196.

Kahlo, "I am really tired . . ." is quoted in Marnham, p. 281.

7. Life's Bitterness

75 Rivera, "acid and tender . . ." is quoted in Wolfe 2000, p. 360.

Kahlo, "I can be free to travel . . ." is quoted in Bambi, June 13, 1954, p. 6C.

Breton, "The art of Frida Kahlo . . ." is from Breton 1996, p. 49.

Breton, "to present interior reality . . ." is from Breton 1978, p. 116.

76 Kahlo, "I never knew I was a Surrealist . . ." is quoted in Wolfe, November 1, 1938, p. 64.

76–77 Levy, "a native Mexican quality . . ." is quoted in Herrera 1983, p. 230.

77 Levy, "mythical creature . . ." is quoted in Herrera 1983, p. 235.

78 Muray, "a contact between people . . ." is quoted in Pomerantz.

    Rivera, "TAKE FROM LIFE . . ." is quoted in Wolfe 2000, p. 359.

79 Kahlo, "I decided to send everything . . ." is from Grimberg, p. 21.

    Kahlo, "s. of a b." is from Grimberg, p. 21.

81 Muray, "Of the three of us . . ." is from Grimberg, p. 25.

    "toad-shaped Mexican muralist . . ." is from *Time*, October 30, 1939, p. 44.

    Rivera, "There is no change . . ." is quoted in *Time*, October 30, 1939, p. 44.

    Kahlo, "We were not getting along well" is quoted in *Art Digest*, p. 8.

85 Rivera, "about the marriage . . ." and "a colossal Goddess . . ." are from *Diego Rivera Mural Project*.

86 Carter, "I remember more than once . . ." is from Carpenter and Totah, p. 52.

    Eloesser, "Diego loves you . . ." is quoted in Herrera 1983, p. 298.

87 Rivera, "was having a bad effect . . ." is from Rivera and March, p. 150.

88 Berggruen, "She was stunning . . ." is quoted in Herrera 1983, p. 300.

    Rivera, "I was so happy . . ." is from Rivera and March, p. 150.

8. Painted Bread

89 Kahlo, "how sweet and good . . ." is from Zamora, p. 113.

90 Kahlo, *I have never seen tenderness* . . . is from Kahlo, p. 247.

    Kahlo, "like an enormous cactus . . ." is from Tibol 1993, pp. 148–49.

    Rivera, "I should have liked much better . . ." is quoted in *Time*, April 4, 1949, p. 64.

    Rivera, "I return to the people . . ." is quoted in *Diego Rivera Museum*, p. 18.

91   Kahlo, "working well" is from Zamora, p. 111.

92-93   Wolfe, "There were monkeys . . ." is quoted in Marnham, p. 305.

93   Kahlo, "Well, kids, I supposedly . . ." is quoted in *Anodis*.

Monroy, "We went to the streets . . ." is quoted in *Anodis*

Estrada, "It was like entering . . ." is quoted in *Anodis*.

94   Rabel, "Everybody loved her . . ." is quoted in Herrera 1983, p. 333.

97   *"Dios No Existe"* is quoted in Stewart, p. 27.

Rivera, "the archbishop bless the building . . ." is quoted in Stewart, p. 29.

Kahlo, "crime against the culture . . ." is from Zamora, p. 138.

97-98   Kahlo, "If you do not act . . ." is from Zamora, pp. 140-41.

98   Chavez, "Diego Rivera is one . . ." is quoted in Stewart, p. 30.

99   Kahlo, "Diego: Nothing compares . . ." is from Kahlo, p. 213.

Kahlo, *Every moment . . .* is from Kahlo, p. 205.

100   Kahlo, *no moon, sun, diamond . . .* is from Kahlo, p. 203.

101   Kahlo, "like a fiesta . . ." is quoted in Bambi, June 16, 1954, p. B3.

9. *Nightfall*

102   Rivera, "dedicated to peace" is quoted in Dellios, p. 2.

104   Rivera, "the best thing I have ever done" is quoted in *Time*, March 17, 1952, p. 64.

Kahlo, "I am a self . . ." and "as the pillars of the new Communist world" are from Kahlo, p. 255.

105   Kahlo, "I crave things . . ." is from Tibol 1977, p. 32.

Kahlo, "for pure pleasure . . ." is quoted in Herrera 1983, p. 403.

Kahlo, "Never again!" is quoted in Herrera 1983, p. 404.

106 Kahlo, *With friendship and love* . . . is from *Frida Kahlo Fans.*

107 Rivera, "Even I was impressed . . ." is from Rivera and March, p. 177.

Child of my heart . . . is quoted in *Time*, April 27, 1953, p. 90.

Rivera, "She must have realized . . ." is from Rivera and March, p. 177.

Kahlo, "I am not sick . . ." is quoted in *Time*, April 27, 1953, p. 90.

Kahlo, "I am DISINTEGRATION," is from Kahlo, p. 225.

108 Kahlo, "Feet what do I need them for . . ." is from Kahlo, p. 274.

Kahlo, "Night is falling in my life" is quoted in Herrera 1983, p. 416.

109 Kahlo, "I hope the leaving is joyful . . ." is from Kahlo, p. 285.

110 Iduarte, "The brilliant and strong-willed creature . . ." is from Iduarte, p. 7.

10. The Great Fiesta

111 Rivera, "Too late now . . ." is from Rivera and March, p. 180.

112 Rivera, "I am a Catholic" is quoted in Hamill, p. 203.

113 Rivera, "I never responded . . ." is from Rivera and March, pp. 119–20.

Murillo (Dr. Atl), "The first thing that strikes us . . ." is from *Testimonios sobre Diego Rivera*, p. 15.

Kahlo, "a great fiesta . . ." is from *Museo Nacional de Artes Plásticas*, p. 39.

113–115 Rivera, "the center of all . . ." is from *Frida Kahlo and Mexican Art*, p. 10.

The Art of Frida Kahlo and Diego Rivera

117 Tibol, "Diego was a deluge . . ." is quoted in Malkin.

Lowe, "Kahlo's self-portraits . . ." is from Lowe, p. 34.

Bibliography

Anodis. *"Pupilos de Frida Kahlo mantienen vivo culto a pintora."* December 10, 2002. URL: anodis.com/nota/561.asp. Downloaded on May 21, 2012.

Apollinaire, Guillaume. *The Cubist Painters.* Translated by Peter Read. Berkeley: University of California Press, 2004.

Art Digest. "Frida vs. Diego." November 1, 1939, p. 8.

Bambi. *"Diego y su vida disipada."* Excelsior, June 16, 1954, pp. 1B, 3B.

———. *"Frida Kahlo es una mitad."* Excelsior, June 13, 1954, pp. 1C, 6C.

Beals, Carleton. *Porfirio Díaz: Dictator of Mexico.* Westport, Conn.: Greenwood Press, 1971.

Breton, André. *El arte de Frida Kahlo es . . . un listó, alrededor de una bomba.* Mexico City: Instituto Nacional de Bellas Artes, 1996.

———. *What Is Surrealism? Selected Writings.* London: Pluto Press, 1978.

Bynner, Witter. *Journey with Genius: Recollections and Reflections Concerning the D. H. Lawrences.* New York: John Day Co., 1951.

Campoy, A. M. *María Blanchard.* Madrid: Editorial Gavar, 1981.

Carmichael, Joel. *Trotsky: An Appreciation of His Life.* New York: St. Martin's Press, 1975.

Carpenter, Patricia F., and Paul Totah, eds. *The San Francisco Fair: Treasure Island, 1939–1940.* San Francisco: Scottwall Associates, 1989.

Las casas de Juan O'Gorman para Diego y Frida. Mexico City: Museo Casa Estudio Diego Rivera y Frida Kahlo, 2001.

Colby, Gerard. *Thy Will Be Done: The Conquest of the Amazon, Nelson Rockefeller and Evangelism in the Age of Oil.* With Charlotte Dennett. New York: Harper & Row, 1976.

Davies, Florence. "Rivera Tells Meaning of Art Institute Murals." *Detroit News,* January 19, 1933, p. 4.

———. "Wife of Master Mural Painter Gleefully Dabbles in Works of Art." *Detroit News,* February 2, 1933, p. 16.

Dellios, Hugh. "Missing Mural Ignites Mexico's Imagination." *Chicago Tribune,* June 1, 2004, pp. 1–2.

Diego Rivera Mural Project, The. URL: www.riveramural.org/home.asp?language=english. Downloaded on May 3, 2012.

Diego Rivera Museum: Anahuacalli. Mexico City: Organizing Committee of the Games of the XIX Olympiad, 1970.

Faure, Élie. *The Italian Renaissance.* London: The Studio, 1929.

Frida Kahlo Fans. "Exposition by Frida Kahlo, April 13th." URL: www.fridakahlofans.com/Kahlo1953Exhibition.html. Downloaded on May 29, 2012.

Grimberg, Salomon. *I Will Never Forget You: Frida Kahlo and Nickolas Muray.* San Francisco: Chronicle Books, 2006.

Hamill, Pete. *Diego Rivera.* New York: Harry N. Abrams, 1999.

Herrera, Hayden. *Frida: A Biography of Frida Kahlo.* New York: Harper & Row, 1983.

———. *Frida Kahlo: The Paintings.* New York: HarperPerennial, 2002.

———. "Portraits of a Marriage." *Connoisseur,* March 1982, pp. 124–28.

Iduarte, Andrés. *"Imagen de Frida Kahlo."* El Nacional (Caracas), special section: *La Vida Humana.* August 12, 1954, p. 7.

Kahlo, Frida. *The Diary of Frida Kahlo: An Intimate Self-Portrait.* New York: Harry N. Abrams, 1995.

Kettenmann, Andrea. *Frida Kahlo, 1907-1954: Pain and Passion*. New York: Barnes and Noble Books, 2004.

Landers, Robert K. *An Honest Writer: The Life and Times of James T. Farrell*. San Francisco: Encounter Books, 2004.

Lilly, Joseph. "Rivera Perpetuates Scenes of Communist Activity for R.C.A. Walls—and Rockefeller, Jr., Foots Bill." *New York World-Telegram*, April 24, 1933, pp. 1, 3.

Lindauer, Margaret A. *Devouring Frida: The Art History and Popular Celebrity of Frida Kahlo*. Hanover, N.H.: Wesleyan/University Press of New England, 1999.

Lisle, Laurie. *Louise Nevelson: A Passionate Life*. New York: Summit Books, 1990.

Lowe, Sarah M. *Frida Kahlo*. New York: Universe Publishing, 1991.

Malkin, Elisabeth. "Rivera, Fridamania's Other Half, Gets His Due." *New York Times*, December 25, 2007. URL: www.nytimes.com/2007/12/25/arts/design/25rive.html?pagewanted=all&r=0. Downloaded on June 18, 2013.

Marnham, Patrick. *Dreaming with His Eyes Open: A Life of Diego Rivera*. New York: Alfred A. Knopf, 1998.

Meyer, Jean A. *The Cristero Rebellion: The Mexican People Between Church and State, 1926-1929*. Cambridge, U.K.: Cambridge University Press, 1976.

Moyssén, Xavier. *La crítica de arte en México, 1896-1921*. Mexico City: Universidad Nacional Autónoma de México, 1999.

Museo Nacional de Artes Plásticas. *Diego Rivera: 50 años de su labor artística*. Mexico City: Departamento de Artes Plásticas, Instituto Nacional de Bellas Artes, 1951.

Nevelson, Louise. *Dawns + Dusks: Conversations with Diana MacKown*. New York: Charles Scribner's Sons, 1976.

New York Herald Tribune. "Rockefeller Center Ousts Rivera and Boards Up Mural." May 10, 1933. URL: xroads.virginia.edu/~MA04/hess/RockRivera/newspapers/NYHerald_05_10_1933.html. Downloaded on April 17, 2012.

Newhall, Nancy, ed. *The Daybooks of Edward Weston*. Vol. 2: *California*. Millerton, N.Y.: Aperture, 1973.

Patenaude, Bertrand M. *Trotsky: Downfall of a Revolutionary*. New York: HarperCollins, 2009.

Pomerantz, James. "Nickolas Muray's Colorful Life." *New Yorker*, October 11, 2011. URL: www.newyorker.com/online/blogs/photobooth/2011/10/nickolas-muray.html. Downloaded on April 22, 2012.

Querido Doctorcito: Frida Kahlo-Leo Eloesser, Correspondencia/Correspondence. Mexico City: DGE Equilibrista: Consejo Nacional para la Cultura y las Artes, 2007.

Rivera, Diego. "Dynamic Detroit — An Interpretation." *Creative Arts*, April 1933, pp. 289–95.

———. "Frida Kahlo and Mexican Art." *The Frida Kahlo Museum*. Mexico City: Comité Organizador de los Juegos de la XIX Olimpiada, 1968, p. 10.

———. *My Art, My Life: An Autobiography*. With Gladys March. New York: Dover Publications, 1991.

———. *Portrait of America*. New York: Covici-Friede, 1934.

———. "Stalin, Undertaker of the Revolution." *Esquire*, May 1940, p. 35, 114.

Rivera Marín, Guadalupe, and Juan Coronel Rivera, comps. *Encuentros con Diego Rivera*. Mexico City: BNCI, 1993.

Rochfort, Desmond. *Mexican Muralists: Orozco, Rivera, Siqueiros*. San Francisco: Chronicle Books, 1998.

Sáenz, Olga. *El símbolo y la acción: Vida y obra de Gerardo Murillo, Dr. Atl*. Mexico City: El Colegio Nacional, 2005.

Shumacker, Harris B. *Leo Eloesser, M.D.: Eulogy for a Free Spirit*. New York: Philosophical Library, 1982.

Smith, F. Hopkinson. *A White Umbrella in Mexico*. Boston: Houghton, Mifflin, 1889.

Stewart, Virginia. *45 Contemporary Mexican Artists: A Twentieth-Century Renaissance.* Stanford, California: Stanford University Press, 1951.

Testimonios sobre Diego Rivera. Mexico City: Universidad Nacional Autónoma de México, 2007.

Thomas, Robert McG., Jr. "Lucienne Bloch, Muralist, Is Dead at 90." *New York Times Biographical Service,* March 1999, p. 422.

Tibol, Raquel. *Escriutas de Frida Kahlo.* Mexico City: Random House Mondadori, 1999.

———. *Frida Kahlo: Crónica, testimonios y aproximaciones.* Mexico City: Ediciones de Cultura Popular, 1977.

———. *Frida Kahlo: An Open Life.* Translated by Elinor Randall. Albuquerque: University of New Mexico Press, 1993.

———, ed. *Frida by Frida.* Chula Vista, Calif.: Trucatriche, 2003.

Time. "Art: Rockefellers v. Rivera." May 22, 1933. URL: xroads.virginia.edu/~MA04/hess/RockRivera/newspapers/Time_05_22_1933.html. Downloaded on April 17, 2012.

Time. "Diego Stays Home." March 17, 1952, p. 64.

Time. "The Long Voyage Home." April 4, 1949, pp. 56–64.

Time. "Mexican Autobiography." April 27, 1953, p. 90.

Time. "Milestones." October 30, 1939, p. 44.

Trotsky, Leon. "Art and Politics." *Partisan Review,* August–September 1938, pp. 3–10.

United Mine Workers of America. *Attempt by Communists to Seize the American Labor Movement.* Washington, D.C.: Government Printing Office, 1924.

Vorobëv, Marevna. *Life in Two Worlds.* Translated by Benet Nash. London: Abelard-Schuman, 1962.

Das Werk des Malers Diego Rivera. Berlin: Neuer Deutscher Verlag, 1928.

Wolfe, Bertram D. *The Fabulous Life of Diego Rivera*. New York: Cooper Square Press, 2000.

———. "Rise of Another Rivera." *Vogue*, November 1, 1938, pp. 64, 131.

Zamora, Martha, comp. *The Letters of Frida Kahlo: Cartas Apasionadas*. San Francisco: Chronicle Books, 1995.

Picture Credits

❀

The art of Frida Kahlo and Diego Rivera appears courtesy of the Diego Rivera Frida Kahlo Museums Trust: © 2012 Banco de México Diego Rivera Frida Kahlo Museums Trust, D.F./ Artists Rights Society (ARS), New York

Frida Kahlo and Diego Rivera, 1931/Paul A. Juley, photographer. Chester Dale papers, Archives of American Art, Smithsonian Institution: cover

Diego Rivera and Frida Kahlo, 1941/Emmy Lou Packard, photographer. Emmy Lou Packard papers, Archives of American Art, Smithsonian Institution: ii

Throckmorton Fine Art: viii

Reproducción Autorizada por el Instituto Nacional de Antropologia e Historia, image 31126. www.fototeca.inah.gob.mx: 2

Frida Kahlo with her painting *Self-Portrait as a Tehuana*, ca. 1943/unidentified photographer. Florence Arquin papers, Archives of American Art, Smithsonian Institution: 3

Diego Rivera working on the *Nightmare of War, Dream of Peace* fresco, 1952/unidentified photographer; Photographs related to Diego Rivera's fresco *The Nightmare of War and the Dream of Peace*, 1952. Archives of American Art, Smithsonian Institution: 5

Archivo Frida Kahlo y Diego Rivera: 9, 10, 23, 26, 31, 112

Library of Congress: 11, 12, 14, 16, 18, 20, 25, 32, 33, 37, 38, 39, 43, 46, 49, 51, 55, 59, 79, 80, 82, 85, 98

Author's collection: 17

Stanford University Medical Center: 47

Lucienne Bloch (1909–1999), courtesy Old State Studios, www.LucienneBloch.com: 53, 61, 63

Louise Nevelson, ca. 1931/unidentified photographer. Louise Nevelson papers, Archives of American Art, Smithsonian Institution: 65

AP/Wide World: 68, 71, 87, 91, 106

Smithsonian American Art Museum, Washington, D.C./Art Resource, N.Y.: 76

AP Photo/Reed Saxon: 83

Frida Kahlo reclining on her bed in Coyoacán, Mexico, between 1942 and 1945/Chester Dale, photographer. Chester Dale papers, Archives of American Art, Smithsonian Institution: 92

Richard Steelman: 94, 114

Frida Kahlo and Diego Rivera in Coyoacán, Mexico, January 1948/Florence Arquin, photographer. Florence Arquin papers, Archives of American Art, Smithsonian Institution: 97

Photofest: 100, 116

Frida Kahlo posing for Diego Rivera while he paints the *Nightmare of War and the Dream of Peace* fresco, 1952; unidentified photographer. Photographs related to Diego Rivera's fresco *The Nightmare of War and the Dream of Peace*, 1952. Archives of American Art, Smithsonian Institution: 103

Frida Kahlo, *Portrait of Alicia Galant (Retrato de Alicia Galant)*, 1927. Oil on canvas; 42 1/2 in. x 36 3/4 in. Collection Museo Dolores Olmedo, Xochimilco, Mexico: 121

Frida Kahlo, *Frieda and Diego Rivera*, 1931. Oil on canvas; 39 3/8 in. x 31 in. (100.01 cm x 78.74 cm) San Francisco Museum of Modern Art, Albert M. Bender Collection, gift of Albert M. Bender: 122

National Museum of Women in the Arts, Washington, D.C., gift of the Honorable Clare Boothe Luce: 123

Harry Ransom Center, University of Texas at Austin: 124, 126

Mary-Anne Martin/Fine Art: 125

National Gallery of Art, Washington, D.C.: 128

Los Angeles County Museum of Art, Los Angeles, Calif., USA. Digital Image © 2013 Museum Associates/LACMA, Licensed by Art Resource, N.Y.: 129, 132

Stock Exchange Tower Associates, *Allegory of California*: 130

Detroit Institute of Arts, USA/Gift of Edsel B. Ford/The Bridgeman Art Library: 131

Image courtesy of City College of San Francisco: 133

Index